John Booth

The Inspector Monde Mysteries

PloxChase Publishing

PfoxChase, a division of Pfoxmoor Publishing
4972 Lowhill Church Road
New Tripoli, PA 18066 USA

www.pfoxmoorpublishing.com
www.pfoxchase.com

The Inspector Monde Mysteries
Copyright ©2011 by John Booth

Print ISBN: 978-1-936827-39-8
Digital ISBN: 978-1-936827-14-5

Cover by Sessha Batto

First Pfoxmoor Publishing electronic publication: June 2011
First Pfoxmoor Publishing print publication: June 2011

Published in the United States of America with international
distribution.

Dedication

To my family and my publisher.
They have a lot to put up with.

Index:

Marie

I

Paris basked in the sun in the spring of 1960. People were beginning to smile again as the French hoped the sixties would bring some relief from the dour fifties. Rationing was becoming a memory and the shops filled with frivolous things as prosperity returned to the city.

Gendarme Louis Bernache walked down the Rue Dante with a bounce to his step. An officer in the Parisian police force for three years he had just achieved his ambition to work in the centre of the city, the place where the action was.

Bernache was a thin man in his early twenties, though he looked younger. He had grown a small moustache for that very reason, to look older. In his crisply starched police uniform, he cut the very figure of the archetypal police officer that makes middle-aged men feel old.

Once inside the police station he approached the small rotund sergeant who stood waiting behind the front desk.

"You'll be Gendarme Bernache then," the sergeant said gruffly before he could speak. "My name is Girard, Sergeant Jacques Girard. We'll soon knock all that youthful optimism out of you. I can't imagine why you were silly enough to transfer from your quiet little station out in the suburbs to here."

Inspector Monde of the Prefecture De Police sat at his desk in that same police station. He hadn't bothered to shed the grey overcoat he wore when he entered the building, but then he almost never did. The Inspector was a tall, thin faced man who looked as if he was in need of a good meal. His complexion was sallow and his eyes sank deep into his skull. He had the look of a man who has seen far too much of both life and death. There were many such men in Paris, striving not to remember the war.

1

Johnny Halliday sang a song about sex and love, with perhaps a little too much emphasis on sex for Inspector Monde's taste. The Inspector listened to the song on a dark brown coloured Bakelite radio, waiting for the hourly news.

It was unusual for the senior members of the French police to listen to the radio while on duty, but Inspector Monde was given more than a little leeway by the Chief Inspector. If he were to resign his post, then who would they give the special cases to? The cases they liked to pretend did not exist.

Inspector Monde turned off the radio when the Chief Inspector entered the room and sat down casually on the edge of Monde's desk. He dropped a set of manila folders in front of Monde. The Inspector picked up and opened the folder on the top of the pile.

"As you can see, Charles, there has been a spate of young men committing suicide by jumping into the Seine," the Chief Inspector pointed out. "Four of them in the last three weeks, to be precise."

"Suicides in the river are nothing new, though they're more common in the autumn and winter, sir," the Inspector replied, flipping through the folders at a breakneck speed. "But I would agree with you, these do look unusual."

"They most certainly are. These particular young men had everything to live for and not one was known to be depressed. You have noted how much alike they look?"

"Their hairstyle has been in fashion since Johnny Halliday took it up. I think it looks better than the Elvis Presley hairstyle. We should not be copying the Americans. Before you know it we'll be following the British in fashion."

"I hardly think that will ever happen," the Chief retorted dryly. "I want you to look into this, Charles. I have a feeling that stopping these deaths will require your special skills."

Inspector Monde looked up at his boss. "I hope you're wrong, sir."

"So do I," the Chief got to his feet and strolled over to the door. "Look into it Charles, and bring it to a close."

Gendarme Bernache and Sergeant Girard watched with open curiosity as the Chief Inspector walked out of Inspector Monde's office.

2

"The one way to be sure that something strange is happening in Paris," Sergeant Girard said sagely to Bernache, "is when the Chief Inspector comes to visit Inspector Monde."

"I don't understand."

"You will if you work in this station for any time. Here's some good advice for you. When you feel the hairs on the back of your neck rising over something, pass the matter on to Inspector Monde as fast as you can."

"I think Inspector Monde looks like he's a good man," Bernache ventured.

"Hah!" Girard snorted. "You'll learn."

It was a warm night, a taste of the summer yet to come. Christian Bideau crushed his cigarette beneath the sole of his black patent leather shoe and entered a seedy little café at the end of a largely unlit street. His shoes made soft smacking sounds on the faded linoleum. Behind a Formica-coated counter, a fat bald man with a cartoon moustache and small piggy eyes looked at him suspiciously. The café was empty except for its owner and a pretty blonde haired girl sat at a small table nursing her coffee.

"Espresso, mon ami," Christian requested and got a shrug of indifference from the café owner for his trouble. The man prepared the drink with the ancient coffee machine behind him and handed it over. Christian laid the appropriate money down on the counter. He picked up the thick syrupy drink and walked over to the girl.

"Do you mind if I sit with you?" he asked. The girl shrugged her indifference.

"I get all the strange ones," the café owner remarked from behind the counter. Christian chose to ignore him.

"I can see you are troubled," the man told the girl. "My name is Christian and yours is…?"

The girl looked up and smiled. It was the sort of smile Cleopatra might have used to launch a thousand ships and Christian felt lust wash over him like a warm wave.

"My boyfriend broke up with me," she said. "See, I have the ring he gave me." She waved a gold ring with a tiny diamond at its centre at Christian. Its position on the third finger of her left hand informed Christian that he had a real chance with her that night, if he was to play his cards right.

3

"How could any man desert a woman as sweet and delectable as you? He must be crazy." Christian said in mock horror. He took the girl's hand and kissed her fingertips softly. The café owner snorted in derision and Christian turned towards him to give him an unfriendly scowl.

The girl giggled and pulled her hand away. "Boys only want one thing."

"And what would that thing be?" Christian asked, arching his eyebrows in feigned puzzlement.

"You know," the girl replied, slapping him lightly on the arm.

"I understand it can be quite pleasurable when it is done right," he remarked before sipping on his coffee. The bitter liquid burnt as it slid down his throat.

"Are you any good at it?"

"I have never had a complaint."

The girl leant over the table until she was inches from Christian's face. "You might get lucky tonight, *if* you are as good as you claim."

"It would be an honour to be your first," Christian replied with straight face and solemn voice.

"It might be a memory you carry to your grave," the girl replied in a whisper. She smiled again and Christian forgot her words. He knew it was pointless to try to make sense of girl's talk. Every man knew that. You agreed with whatever mad thought they came up with until you flattered them into your arms.

"I have a special place I go when I'm feeling romantic," the girl said suggestively. Christian realised that she still hadn't told him her name. But then he thought, who cared? At least this way, he couldn't be accused of forgetting it.

"Would you like to go there now?" he asked.

"Let us do just that."

The girl stood up. She allowed Christian to open the café door for her. As soon as she was out of the door, she started running down the street. "You must catch me first!" she yelled at him. Christian began to give chase.

They ended up on one of the older bridges over the river Seine. The bridge was a stone monstrosity left over from a previous century. There were semi-circular areas away from the road where you could stand and watch the river drift by. The river looked cold and black in the light of the lanterns lighting the bridge.

There had once been iron railings to stop people falling over the low stone parapet. At some point in the war, the railings were cut off to help the war effort. The German war effort of course, Paris and France fell disturbingly easily to the blitzkrieg. To France's eternal shame, they hadn't even fired a single shot.

The girl laughed as he pinned her against the bridge wall. He leant forward so her head and back hung over the river before finding her lips. He was surprised at how cold her lips tasted. It was as if the run had cooled her down. Christian slipped his arms around her and caressed her thigh. She responded to him with surprising passion.

The girl pushed him away from her and spun him around. Christian found that the wall was not very high, only reaching up to the top of his legs.

"Do you want me?" the girl said as she pressed her body hard against his. In the near darkness, his senses were overwhelmed by her sensuous touch. Christian felt her unbutton his flies. He had no desire to resist her advances, she was a dream come true.

She pushed harder against him and still felt cold, but there could be no denying how urgent her need had become. Christian held her tight as he pressed his body closer against her. She lifted her skirt and he slid inside her.

Christian found the girl edging him further over the wall. It was as if she had acquired the strength of a tiger. Only the fact he was holding her prevented him falling off the bridge and down to a watery grave. He found the feeling intensely stimulating and moaned with pleasure, unable to hold back his climax.

The girl slipped from his grasp, though he could have sworn he held her tightly. Unbalanced he flapped his arms to prevent himself from falling. The girl gave him a gentle push over the wall, her face glowing with anger.

"See what it feels like!" she screamed as he began the long fall into the river below.

II

Louis Bernache was having trouble at the front desk. Sergeant Girard was at lunch as were nearly all the other officers and he wasn't sure what he should do. A young woman berated him, the police and Parisians in general, for not taking her seriously.

Beneath her elegant exterior Bernache felt the woman was holding back an icy rage. It frightened him with its intensity. He was sure she was more than capable of committing murder to get what she wanted. In five minutes of conversation, he hadn't managed to obtain much in the way of details about her complaint. In desperation, he remembered what Sergeant Girard had advised him and looked toward Inspector Monde's closed office door.

Inspector Monde sat at his desk reading the reports on the suicides for the fiftieth time. He knew he should be out taking statements but something seemed to be holding him in the office. He just wasn't sure what. It was as though he was waiting for something to happen.

A young gendarme Monde didn't recognise opened his office door after a single knock. Whoever the gendarme was, he gave Monde the impression of being harassed and out of his depth.

"Gendarme Bernache, sir. I have a young lady who is determined to talk to someone in authority about her missing sister. I know you're working on the suicides, but if you could see her…?"

"Send her in, Bernache. In any case, I am getting nowhere with my investigations at the moment." Monde gave the gendarme a friendly smile. Bernache heaved a sigh of relief.

A striking blonde haired girl in her early twenties stormed into Monde's office. She pushed past Bernache as though he was a piece of furniture. Inspector Monde waved her towards the plastic tubular steel chair in front of his desk and the girl sat down on it.

"What can I do for you, mademoiselle…?"

"Madeleine, Madeleine Poussier. It is about my sister, Marie. She's been missing for nearly a month now and the police have done nothing about it."

6

Inspector Monde put up his hand to stop her tirade of words.

"Perhaps, if you were to tell me about it from the beginning?"

Madeleine composed herself, smoothing down her skirt and clamping her knees firmly together. She looked deep into the Inspector's eyes and started again.

"I have a younger sister, Marie. She is seventeen, four years younger than me, though many people say we look almost identical, as though we were twins."

"Then she must be very beautiful."

Madeleine looked uncomfortable at the compliment. After a brief pause she continued with her story.

"Marie was engaged to be married to a most unsuitable young man, Bernard Holcanruy. I told her and told her she was too young, but she would not listen to me. I am Marie's only family as our parents were killed during the liberation and our grandmother died last year." Madeleine paused for breath.

"So I take it you are her legal guardian?"

"Exactly so. Bernard broke up with her four weeks ago and fled to Cannes where he has relatives. Marie became hysterical and disappeared a few days later. I thought at first she was staying with friends to avoid hearing me say 'I told you so', but I have not seen her since."

"And you believe that something may have happened to her?" Monde was wondering if he should order some coffee when there was a knock at the door and Bernache entered with two cups of coffee on a metal tray.

Madeleine waited until the gendarme left the room before she answered the Inspector's question.

"I've had a bad feeling ever since she disappeared. Bernard was far from being a suitable young man, though I could not convince Marie of it. Men like him should be shot, for they do nothing but seek gratification by taking advantage of young women. I worry Marie is roaming the streets in a distraught state or that she may have fallen into the thrall of dubious people. I'm worried about her Inspector, but no one is willing to take me seriously."

"Perhaps she has followed this man of hers. Bernard, you said his name was. She may be with him in Cannes, even as we speak," the Inspector suggested.

"That was what the other policemen suggested. I have sent several telegrams to his family and they have categorically denied she is with him." Madeleine responded in annoyance. "I am not a fool, Inspector."

"I would never suggest such a thing. Do you have a photograph of Marie I might borrow?"

"I have one." Madeleine said and offered up a small black and white snapshot showing a girl the Inspector might well have assumed was Madeleine herself. The girl in the picture was laughing, standing arm in arm with a similarly happy young man.

"Is this man Bernard?"

"Yes, though that picture was taken a year ago and he looks different now."

"In what way?" Monde asked, taking a bet on the answer she would give.

"He has a different haircut now. Like that insipid ballad singer, you know the one?"

"Johnny Halliday?"

"Yes, that's the one."

The Inspector put the photograph inside a manila folder along with his notes of the meeting. "Leave it to me. Give your contact details to the gendarme who brought you to me and I'll be in touch shortly. I can assure you I will not leave a stone unturned in my search for your sister."

When Madeleine left his office, the Inspector took the picture and compared the young man's face to that of the drowned men. They looked like him more than they looked like each other. Bernard Holcanruy was the common factor between these men, he was certain.

The Inspector wondered about Madeleine's state of mind. Despite the fact that she had been articulate when talking to him, she also appeared to be nearing a nervous breakdown. She undoubtedly hated young men like Bernard Holcanruy, a fact he could hardly dismiss out of hand.

The Central Morgue was not a pleasant place to visit. It reminded the Inspector of swimming baths without the water. White tiles rose from floor to ceiling on all sides. He was in a room that was almost below ground. Small frosted glass windows just below the ceiling on one wall let in a little light from the street.

The Inspector stood on large marble floor tiles designed to be washed easily. The floor sloped towards a tiny drain covered with an iron grill. The whole place stank of carbolic soap and below that smell, but still recognisable, was the sickly sweet odour of recent death.

Dr Jean-Paul DePaul was a wizened old man who looked as though he should have retired years ago. As chief pathologist for Paris he always became involved in cases where the body count was high.

The Inspector and Jean-Paul had known each other for a long time and the Inspector could see that Jean-Paul was bothered by something. They stood beside a marble slab on which lay the body of a young man. He had been found floating in the Seine that morning and was the first new victim since Inspector Monde took over the case.

Jean-Paul pulled away the white shroud covering the body, revealing a man remarkably similar in features to all the others that had died.

"Something is bothering you, Jean-Paul?" the Inspector asked. He could see nothing unusual about this particular body, but he trusted his friend's instincts.

"This one is like all the others," Jean-Paul replied.

"I suspect the killer is selecting young men who look similar."

"There is no evidence of murder," Jean-Paul retorted. "These men died as a result of drowning. The river flows cold and fast at this time of the year and even the strongest swimmer would soon succumb to it."

"Most of the victims show the signs of striking the water from a great height, which I doubt helped their survival chances." Jean-Paul remarked. "However, it was not their physical appearance that I was referring to. All young men look the same to me these days."

"If not their looks, then what?" the Inspector asked, surprised that there might be another common factor.

"I cannot be certain that it is anything. A drowning man will thrash and struggle and it is not unusual to find them drifting and parted from their clothes, or for their clothes to be in a state of disarray when we drag them out."

9

"Get to the point man," the Inspector said sharply, annoyed at his friend's prevarication.

"All these men were found undressed to some extent. This one's fly buttons were undone. Two of them were found without trousers and one with his trousers wrapped around his ankles. The other body was like this one, fly buttons undone."

"Are you suggesting that these young men were pushed into the river while relieving themselves?" Inspector Monde asked.

"There is more than one kind of relief that requires the trousers to be down or undone," Jean-Paul reminded him sarcastically.

Emile Fornier stood behind the counter of his café and scowled at Inspector Monde. "All young men look the same these days with their fancy hairstyles and stupid clothes. And they are all crazy. I see them talking to themselves and laughing without reason."

The Inspector noted Emile's bald head and discounted his comment about hairstyles. His investigations led him to believe that all five of the dead young men frequented this particular café prior to their deaths. The café owner was not proving a reliable witness though, as he appeared to believe the young men were acting crazy when they entered his premises.

The Inspector realised he was going to have to stake out this café until another victim appeared. He groaned at the thought. Even though the weather had been extraordinarily mild during the last few weeks, it was still only the beginning of April and most of the nights were wet and cold.

Somebody would notice if he parked his car across the street. Even the more honest citizens of Paris spotted them regularly. The Inspector knew he would have to go unnoticed if his stakeout was to work. He was just going to have to stand in a doorway all night.

III

The acrid white smoke from the last of Inspector Monde's cigarettes curled around his head. Winter made an unwelcome return during the night and a sheen of ice covered the paving stones. There was little street lighting and the only things lit up were the windows of Emile Fornier's Midnight Café. It stood out in the night as a beacon of warmth and life.

Inspector Monde stood in the doorway from eight in the evening until the first light of dawn for three nights. He was amazed Fornier made any kind of a living because there had been few customers on any of the nights.

As he stamped his feet against the cold, the Inspector wondered if he had it wrong about the café. He supposed that the next body found in the river would tell him, one way or the other.

The Inspector could have sworn no one entered the café, but a blonde haired girl was sitting at the table farthest from the door. She nursed a cup of coffee in her hands but showed no sign of drinking it. From where the Inspector stood, he could not be certain if it was Madeleine or Marie Poussier; the two sisters were so similar in appearance. But it was certainly one of them.

Emile Fornier ignored the girl, which was unusual behaviour on his part. The man had repeatedly displayed lecherous tendencies during Monde's stakeout. The Inspector had seen two girls walk out in disgust after making the mistake of buying a coffee while alone in that café.

Inspector Monde tossed a mental coin and decided speaking to the girl outweighed watching what she did next. If it was Marie, then he could put her sister's mind at rest. If it was Madeleine, well that would open up another line of enquiry. Monde dropped his cigarette and crushed it. He needed to buy another packet of cigarettes anyway.

The little bell above the café door tinkled as Monde pushed it open. A wave of warm air hit him and he realised just how cold it had been outside.

11

"Shut the damned door!" Emile snarled and Monde pushed it closed. The girl looked up from her coffee. She took a quick look at Monde and looked away.

"Twenty Gitanes and a coffee," Monde informed Emile. The Inspector could tell Emile hadn't recognised him from his visit earlier in the week. That suited the Inspector so he made no effort to remind the café owner of who he was.

Emile placed the hot cup of coffee in front of the Inspector and the doorbell tinkled again. Monde spun around, seeing the girl had gone. He ran to the door, opened it and stared out into the night. There was no sign of her.

Returning to Emile, he flashed his identity card at him. Emile's face paled as he recognised the Inspector.

"How many times has that girl come in here?" Monde asked. He was annoyed with himself for not going straight over to her.

"What girl?" Emile asked, looking puzzled.

"The one sitting at that table, drinking that coffee," the Inspector replied, pointing at the cup and saucer.

"I served that to a man about an hour ago," Emile replied. "I often don't bother cleaning up until the morning. I don't get enough customers for it to be a problem."

Monde walked over to the cup and put his finger into the dregs. The liquid in the cup was cold.

"I must have been mistaken."

The Inspector drank his coffee slowly before going home to bed.

"Swing the weights over more to the right!" a burly man in a donkey jacket shouted. A couple of similarly dressed men attempted to throw weights attached to a thick rope net further out into the river.

Inspector Monde was surprised they weren't using boats, but the supervisor of the team assured him they wouldn't be necessary. The Seine curved at this point and much of its flotsam and jetsam ended up here.

"I can't see the point of this," Gendarme Bernache complained. Inspector Monde had Bernache assigned to him this morning and had decided working out in the field would be good for the young gendarme. It was always difficult for the Inspector to retain the men, they tended to request transfers after one or two cases. The

Inspector wondered if Bernache would stay longer than the others if he gave him enough interesting things to do.

"I have reason to believe we will find a body here," the Inspector explained patiently.

"All the other bodies were floating," Bernache pointed out.

"All the bodies we know about."

There was a shout from one of the men. There had been other shouts that morning and they already had a pram, two bicycles and part of a street lamp in a growing collection on the bank. The Inspector looked over without any great expectations as a large muddy object was pulled up into the air and swung towards the riverbank. Chunks of river mud fell away as the object cleared the river to reveal dangling bloated human legs.

"Sacre Bleu!" Gendarme Bernache said, crossing himself.

Dr Jean-Paul DePaul sighed as Inspector Monde walked into his office.

"We have only had the body for four hours Charles. You know I hate to rush an autopsy."

"Lives are at stake here, Jean-Paul. You know I would not press you otherwise."

"The body is that of a young woman, in her late teens, a natural blonde. Her body is badly decomposed and I cannot be sure how long she has been in the water. I am certain she was murdered. Her hands were tied behind her back."

"That is usually a fairly clear indication," the Inspector agreed.

Her clothes are in a better state than she is and there were bricks in her coat pockets. She was pregnant. Only a few months, it would not have been showing, but she would have known." Jean-Paul sighed yet again. "Such a tragedy"

"Is there anything else you can tell me?" the Inspector asked gently.

"Her hands were tied behind her back as I said, but there was one other unusual thing." Jean-Paul paused.

"Well?"

"Her right fingers were grasping one of her left ones. The grip was so tight that we had to cut her right fingers away to see what she was grasping."

"And?" the Inspector demanded impatiently.

13

"It was the third finger of her left hand, and what she was holding was her engagement ring. I think she was trying to tell us something as she died, don't you?"

"Bernard Holcanruy, I presume?" Inspector Monde asked, as two burly gendarmes dragged a handcuffed young man into a cell in the police station basement.

"This is an outrage," Bernard snarled. "I've been dragged back here from Cannes against my will. This is all that bitch Madeleine's fault."

Bernard looked just like his picture except for his hairstyle. In the Inspector's view, Johnny Halliday had a lot to answer for.

"I believe you can help me with my enquiries into the disappearance of Marie Poussier."

The gendarmes pushed Bernard down into the chair in front of a small table. One of them unlocked Bernard's handcuffs and then locked them again so he was fastened to the chair with his hands held behind his back. Inspector Monde waved the two men out of the room.

"We will be just down the corridor, Inspector. In the event that you should require any assistance," said the taller of the two gendarmes.

Inspector Monde walked around to the front the table and sat on the corner of it, looking at Bernard in curiosity. Before he could ask a question, Bernard launched into a defensive tirade.

"I don't know where Marie is. Ask her sister, she spied on the two of us all the time and followed us everywhere. Is it any wonder I left Marie? I had left for Cannes before she disappeared."

"And exactly when did Marie disappear?"

"It was on the Wednesday night. I left for Cannes on the preceding Monday."

"I have copies of the telegrams Madeleine Poussier sent you and your relatives here," the Inspector handed over three pieces of paper to Bernard. "Perhaps you can show me where it says Marie went missing on a Wednesday?"

Bernard's face paled. "She must have told me later."

"Madeleine was not certain her sister was missing until several days after you drowned her in the river," Inspector Monde explained. "I suppose that when Marie told you she was pregnant

14

you had to get rid of her. That or do the decent thing and marry her."

"You can't prove I killed her!" Bernard screamed.

"I am sure I can. I have a witness who saw the two of you together on Wednesday night. Two nights after you claim you left for Cannes. Not to mention the evidence from Marie herself, of course. Her body was found clutching her engagement ring in a death grip. No jury in France will find you innocent on evidence like that."

"I told her it was over and then the bitch told me she was pregnant! I've another girl I'm in love with."

"I'm sure that will be of comfort to you as you make the walk to the guillotine," the Inspector retorted dryly. "You have no concept of what you have done, do you?"

"She told me she was pregnant," Bernard repeated in a whisper. "What choice did I have?"

"Bernard, before I leave. I want you to tell me exactly where you pushed Marie into the river. Lives depend on it."

Bernard shook his head, determined to tell the Inspector nothing more. Monde took out a cosh from his coat and slapped it into his hand. It was not enough simply to threaten, but Inspector Monde had the information he required within the hour.

"Why is the Inspector interviewing that man in the cells rather than his office?" Bernache asked Sergeant Girard as the two men stood behind the front desk.

The Sergeant gave Bernache a piercing look as he suspected at first that the young gendarme was winding him up. However, from the look on Bernache's face, it was clear to him the young gendarme was simply naïve.

"I believe the Inspector needs some information the prisoner will be reluctant to supply without persuasion," Girard replied dryly.

Bernache looked uncomfortable as understanding dawned on him. "Is that not against the law?"

"Inspector Monde most certainly believes in justice. However, I have never been fully convinced he believes in the law."

The weather had turned warm again. The night was balmy as Inspector Monde stood looking down over the edge of the bridge into the river below. The Seine swirled darkly past.

The Inspector was waiting to see if the girl would turn up this night. The only way to end this string of murders was to catch the murderer red handed. She had to be told what had happened to Bernard.

Cold strong hands caught him around the waist. They were much stronger than he expected and there was no possibility at all that he could break free of them. He felt himself being pushed over the wall. Her fury was greater than he anticipated.

"Bernard has been arrested. He will be executed. I promise you."

The girl's hands held the Inspector just as firmly as before, but he was no longer over the edge.

"It is over, little one, you need do nothing more. I understand the tragedy you have endured. You must stop now, it is over."

He felt her body press against his as she suddenly hugged him tightly. He felt her tears soak into his shirt. She spoke in a whisper.

"It is over. It can be over now that bastard will die."

She hugged him, so tight the Inspector barely could breathe.

Then her grip slackened.

He whispered 'Marie' as he turned around. But Marie was gone.

The bridge stood silent and empty except for the Inspector, who looked at the cold dark stone and the lights of the city.

To Inspector Monde, the bridge felt suddenly empty of grace.

The End

Missing

I

Inspector Monde looked out of his window onto the grey and somewhat grubby street below. Parisians have a special love of dogs and several elegant looking people were walking their canine companions along the pavements besides the parked cars. Charles Monde sighed with resignation as a woman let her dog relieve himself against the front door of the Inspector's car. Perhaps, the Inspector thought, I can get Gendarme Bernache to throw a bucket of water over my car, or even the woman and her dog if he can get out there fast enough.

Louis Bernache was the gendarme Inspector Monde had come to rely on over the last few months. Bernache was a young man in his early twenties with very nearly jet black hair plastered to his head with oil and a similarly coloured small moustache under his nose.

Bernache was still young enough to be awed at the thought of working for an inspector and still inexperienced enough to have not realised how unusual Inspector Monde's cases were. Despite his fear of corpses, he had proved to be a willing assistant and Monde was going to miss him when he requested a transfer. All Monde's assistants requested a transfer, sooner or later.

Two young children wearing clothes more typical of the 1940's than the last few years walked up to the faded black doors of the police station. The solid outer doors were latched open and the children walked through them to push the glazed inner doors that opened into the body of the police station.

"What do you two want?" Sergeant Girard asked gruffly. Jacques Girard was usually a jolly man, but for some reason the sight of these two children upset him. He stared at them belligerently, hoping to scare them both away.

The boy looked to be younger than the girl, who herself appeared to be no more than ten years old. Their clothes were old fashioned but not that unusual in Paris where there were still many people passing clothes down from generation to generation until they were worn out. The children looked as though they had gotten dressed in a hurry. The boy's shirt was buttoned up one hole wrong and the girl's dress was only loosely fastened with a knot rather than a bow.

The boy carried a small teddy bear by its threadbare arm. The arm looked as though it was going to come off at any second. They were presentable enough children, but for some reason they chilled the sergeant. Perhaps it was the wide-eyed and unblinking way they stared at him.

"They have stolen dear mama and we must get her back," the little girl told him in a taut and prim little voice.

"Who has stolen your mother? Do you mean you've become separated from her in the streets?"

"Do not be foolish, gendarme," the little boy replied, just as primly as his sister. Indeed, there may well have been an element of contempt in his tone. "Anne-Laure explained it clearly. Mama has been taken and we would like her to be returned. Right this minute, if you please."

An hour later, Sergeant Girard knocked at Inspector Monde's office door.

"Enter."

"I am sorry to bother you Inspector but we have a bit of a problem in the interview room."

Inspector Monde raised an eyebrow. It was more than a little unusual for the capable sergeant to seek his help, especially about an interview.

"Perhaps you would care to explain?"

"We have two young children, aged ten and eight. A boy and a girl, in fact. They say their names are Pierre-Louis and Anne-Laure Charbonneau," Sergeant Girard explained.

"I'm grateful for that information sergeant. However, I do not see how these facts merit my attention. Are you incapable of dealing with a couple of children?"

"They claim they have lost their mother and that we have taken her. I have phoned all the nearby police stations and no one has detained a woman called Charbonneau. When I asked the children for their address, they gave me a nonsense one. Perhaps you can help me with them?"

"In what way was the address nonsense?"

"The address they gave was 147b Rue De Maison. That is where the flats used to be before they were burnt to the ground during the war. It is a building site at the moment as workmen are clearing the rubble prior to rebuilding. No one has lived there since 1942."

The Inspector gave a small jolt at the address, as though he had been stung. He thought about what he had just been told.

"You think these children are making fun of you, sergeant?"

"I don't know what to think. They seem sincere. They claim that we've taken their mother and they appear to be upset." The sergeant did not speak the final part of his appeal, that it was Inspector Monde who took all such cases.

"Call the appropriate child services for me and get someone to come down. These children will need somewhere to spend the night until we can locate a parent. I will go and speak to them. Please ask Gendarme Bernache to join me in the interview room, Sergeant."

"Thank you, Inspector," Sergeant Girard replied with evident relief. The children had bothered him and he was very glad to be rid of them.

II

When Inspector Monde entered the interview room, he found the children standing together, side by side, almost as if they were standing at attention. Their eyes were focused on the door and as soon as he entered through it, their eyes transferred to him.

"At last," the girl exclaimed as if she were a school teacher and he the tardy pupil. "I was beginning to think there was no one in this place who could possibly understand."

"Understand what?" Inspector Monde asked her mildly.

"'They have stolen our dear Mama from us. She is ours forever and you can't have her. Please help us to find her, for we cannot endure the loss." Anne-Laure's voice broke a little, as if she was about to burst into tears. Her brother, Pierre-Louis, nodded his head vigorously in his agreement with her sentiment.

The Inspector knelt down so his eyes were level with the two children. "I promise you I will find your mother and take you to her. It may take me a little time to do that, so you will have to be patient with me. Will you do that for me children? Will you be patient?"

Anne-Laure studied the Inspector's face carefully for signs of deception. After a few moments, she smiled briefly. "I believe you will do it for us, Inspector. We will be patient for a while, but do not keep us waiting too long."

Louis Bernache chose that moment to enter the room. Both children stepped backwards placing their backs against the wall. Bernache noted their reaction with surprise. He usually got on well with young children and wasn't used to them being frightened of him.

"Children, this is my colleague, Louis Bernache. You share a name with him Pierre. I want you to give Louis a full description of your mother and to tell him all about where you live."

The Inspector motioned to Bernache that he wanted a private word with him outside the room. The two men withdrew from the children and the Inspector closed the door behind them so they could not be overheard. He spoke so quietly to Bernache that the man had to move closer so he could hear.

"Do not contradict anything these children tell you, just write it down. Under no circumstances, are you to tell them that what they are telling you is in any way in error. Do you understand?"

"Yes Inspector, but why...?"

"I want you to stay here with them until someone arrives to take them for the night. Sergeant Girard is arranging that as we speak. I have to go out now and may not be back for some time."

"Where are you going, Inspector, if I may ask?"

"I am going to take a walk back in time. I used to live on the Rue de Maison I haven't been back there for a long, long time, but I think I have to do so now."

"Isn't that where...?" Bernache realised he had said too much and didn't finish his sentence.

"Yes Louis, it is where my wife died. I am surprised you know so much."

"I wanted to know more about you, sir. I didn't mean any harm by it," Bernache explained uneasily.

"I understand. Look after these children for me. Listen carefully to what they tell you."

The Inspector turned from Bernache and walked down the corridor without a backward glance.

Inspector Monde walked with his hands thrust deep into the pockets of his overcoat, his head down and his shoulders hunched. He walked down the Rue de Maison and past the last of the shops coming onto the section of road where the devastation lay uncleared from the war. There were very few of these places left in Paris and even the buildings here were being demolished in preparation for new flats. He should have been happy to see the work taking place but somehow he wasn't.

A linked wire fence had been erected by the builders to keep the local children off the site while demolition and clearance took place. The heavy machinery stood silent, the workers having finished for the night. A hint of diesel from the stilled bulldozers and crane fragranced the air with its sweet perfume.

Monde peered through the fence, trying to remember the sights and sounds of the past. He and his wife lived here for a while, before she was shot by the Nazi's for being a member of the Resistance. She had been dragged down this road screaming abuse at her captors. Monde fled for his life. He had never forgiven himself for that, for not staying in an attempt to save her and running away. It was the reason he hadn't walked down this road from that day to this. He felt it had not yet been long enough.

An old man wearing a thick muffler and heavy coat stood close to an oil drum, holes knocked through its sides so it could serve as a makeshift stove. A fire burned merrily inside it, flames licked out through the holes.

"Good evening," the Inspector said. "Are you the watchman?"

"I've no other reason for being here. Nothing worth stealing here though, I can tell you, it was all burnt to ash long ago. I lost a leg during the war, but I can still keep kids from playing in the rubble." The man coughed into his muffler.

"I lost a wife," the Inspector said under his breath, too low to be heard.

"What?" the man said leaning closer.

"I'm sorry. I said that there may still be bodies under the rubble."

"Skeletons are all we find. Flesh long rotted away or eaten by the rats," the watchman said cheerfully. "Nobody cares much. They just ship them over to the morgue when they find them."

Inspector Monde offered the man a cigarette, which was taken gratefully. He lit one for himself after he lit the watchman's cigarette with a long match. The sulphurous smoke from the match drifted in front of him and he waved it away.

"Have you found any recently?"

"One over there," the watchman said, pointing into the distance. "We found it yesterday, God rest its soul. Must have been in a basement flat, given it was below ground level. Would you like to have a look before the light fades?"

"That would be most generous of you."

Monde and the night watchman picked their way carefully through the smashed bricks and lumps of mortar towards a large pit. Inspector Monde peered over the edge and saw an old floor, strewn with rubble, about eight feet below where they were standing. Looking carefully, he could see the remains of an old kitchen range and bits of furniture among all the detritus.

"Do they know who the skeleton was?"

"Not a clue, all the records are gone and many people moved in and out of these buildings. The Nazi records say it was a place the Resistance gathered and they were happy to see it razed." The watchman coughed, "I was in the resistance, lost my leg fighting the Nazi's."

Inspector Monde smiled. If you took all the people in Paris who claimed they had been in the Resistance and counted them, you would end up with ten times more people than were in the French Resistance at its height. The ones who really were in the resistance never spoke of it.

"Then you should have another cigarette my friend, for your service to France." The Inspector proffered his packet and then tossed it lightly into the man's hand. "In fact, take the lot, if you would do me a small favour."

"Anything legal," the old man said. "The pay of a night watchman will barely feed a cat, let alone pay for cigarettes."

The Inspector offered the man his card. "Tomorrow morning, when the manager of this site arrives, give him this card. Tell him I require him to stop work on this site until he has spoken to me. Can I trust you to pass on this message?"

"Yes sir, Monsieur Inspector. He will not be happy though. His men are paid not by the hours they put in but by how much they accomplish," the watchman said respectfully. It paid to be respectful to the police.

"I will not delay him long, and I am always in my office from very early in the morning. Goodnight to you, sir."

Louis Bernache liked to get into the police station early and he was there by half-past six the next morning. Inspector Monde was already at his desk working. This was not a surprise. Louis Bernache half believed his superior didn't sleep and came back to his office to work once everyone from the dayshift left. There were many stories told about Inspector Monde behind his back. None of the stories were the kind you could repeat to the Inspector's face.

"Do you have the children's statements?" Monde enquired as soon as his assistant had taken off his hat and coat.

"Yes sir, but I have not had time to type them up." Bernache reached for his notebook.

"Come into my office and give me the gist of it then."

Bernache sat in the plastic chair in front of the Inspector's desk while the inspector sat behind his desk and stared at the ceiling as if deep in thought.

"The children's names are Pierre-Louis Charbonneau aged eight and Anne-Laure Charbonneau aged ten. They claim they live at 147b Rue De Maison, which is preposterous."

"The 'b' in that address would imply that it was a basement flat," the Inspector remarked.

"Some places do that, for other addresses it simply means a house address was broken into parts when they turned it into flats," Bernache pointed out.

"But in the flats in the Rue De Maison it always meant that the address was a basement flat," The Inspector said in a matter of fact way. Bernache shrugged, he couldn't see what difference it made, as an imaginary address was still an imaginary address, even if it was below ground.

"Did they give you the name of their mother?" The Inspector enquired.

"Marie-Amable Charbonneau, a common enough name. There are twenty two of them in the central Paris telephone book."

The Inspector raised his eyebrows.

"I counted them sir, as I rang each and every one of them last night."

"Well done, Louis. That was good thinking, even if it was doomed to fail. What of the children's father?"

"Died in a rail accident, according to the children. Again, I can find no trace of such an accident." Bernache looked hard at the inspector. "Those two children made me feel uneasy, but I never thought for a minute they were lying. It is possible they are mentally ill?"

"Tell me what they said about their mother's disappearance?" the Inspector asked, totally ignoring Bernache's question. "Their exact words, if you have them written down."

Bernache consulted his notebook and read from it, his finger moving along the line of text to make sure he did not misquote the words.

"This was from the girl.'They came and took her away from us. It isn't fair; we have been together for so long'. Then the boy said 'We will be angry if the Inspector fails us. We have a right to stay together'."

"They do have such a right Bernache. I have seen enough in my life to avoid getting on the wrong side of children such as these. They could prove difficult to deal with."

Anything further he might have said was lost as the telephone on his desk rang. Like all the inspectors in the police force, he had his own private line. He picked up the phone and listened.

"I understand, but what I want should not delay you much. Simply search in the same area looking under debris. You will know what I want when you find them. Yes, two of them, I believe."

The Inspector put down the phone and turned to Bernache. "I have an important task for you, Bernache. I need you to contact the Cardinal of Paris, the Commissioner de Police and the Chief Inspector. Tell them I need them to arrange to meet me at the

Central Morgue, tonight at nine. Once you have done that, arrange for the children to be brought there at nine-thirty, not before."

Bernache looked at the Inspector incredulously. He realised his mouth was open and shut it with an audible click. "Is there a problem, Bernache?" the Inspector enquired innocently.

"I'm not sure such important people will come at such short notice," Bernache stated.

"They will for me, Bernache. I want you there as well. It is only appropriate that you should be there at the end."

"I will do my best, Inspector," Bernache said, saluting his inspector smartly.

"I am sure your best will be more than adequate," The Inspector remarked. "If anybody wants to contact me, I will be at the Central Morgue."

Inspector Monde helped his old friend Dr Jean-Paul DePaul to arrange the bones on the slabs. They had just received two muslin sacks from the building site and there was a lot of sorting to do.

"Charles, I do believe you will be the death of me," Jean-Paul said as he carefully placed a jawbone just below the skull on his slab. "I plan to come back and haunt you for all the things you have put me through. You realise that, don't you?"

"I look forward to it, my old friend. Provided you are willing to help me out on the odd enquiry. I could do with someone helping from the other side."

"You are incorrigible, Charles. No other inspector de police has me rushing around putting old bones into place, just so he can stage a movie style dénouement." Jean Paul complained. His complaining didn't slow his hands down in placing the bones.

"It is necessary. You know I would normally sort out this kind of thing without involving anybody, but there are official records now. Questions would be asked in high places, not to mention the questions the nuns at Our Blessed Mary's Orphanage ask."

"I am a rational man, Charles," Jean-Paul said, his hands shaking a little as he considered what was soon to come. "However, a man of science should have nothing to do with you. You are far too disturbing to be around."

"You need not stay, old friend. I only need you to arrange the bones as a matter of respect for the dead."

"And miss this? I have a suspicion that our Cardinal Lévesque the Archbishop of Paris is also a rational man, and I want to watch his face as you play out your game. He has never met you, has he?" Monde gave a small shake of his head. "His predecessor told me he dreaded your calls, and he was of the old school, a true believer." Jean-Paul had a wicked grin on his face, quite inappropriate for a doctor getting on in years. "This promises to be fun!"

"One minute you are telling me that your heart will not stand the strain, the next how much you are looking forward to it. Make up your mind Jean-Paul," Monde said in exasperation. The exasperation was caused by not knowing if the bone he held was from an arm or a leg. Jean-Paul took the bone from his hand and put it down in the correct place.

"It is like going on a fairground ride, Charles. It is both at once. If I am to die from a heart attack or if I was to forever regret missing this event, either way the fault would be yours."

"Thank you old friend, I love you too."

"It is done," Jean-Paul said with satisfaction as he looked down at the mortuary slabs. "A few bones are missing, but what else would you expect? Will it meet the need?"

"It will have to," the Inspector replied and sighed.

III

At nine o'clock in the evening, the doors to the morgue opened and Chief Inspector Antoine Tessier, Cardinal Lévesque and the Commissioner de Police walked into the room followed by an awed Louis Bernache. He stayed as far in the background as he possibly could while remaining in the room.

Cardinal Lévesque looked more than a little irritated and as soon as they got into the room, he launched into a loud tirade.

"Why have I been summoned here by a lowly Inspector? I am the Archbishop of Paris and the most senior Cardinal in the whole of France. My secretary informed me that I must come to your call and I would like to know why."

The Commissioner de Police reached over to the Cardinal and patted him on the shoulder sympathetically. "I know it seems strange, Philippe, but there is one Inspector in Paris for whom the normal rules do not apply. I would like to introduce you to Inspector Charles Monde who handles some of our more delicate investigations." The Commissioner looked meaningfully at Monde. "I know he would not bring us out here unnecessarily, especially as it is making me late for the opera. Inspector Monde knows full well how much the opera means to my lady wife."

Inspector Monde did indeed know full well how much the Commissioner's wife loved the opera. He also knew that the Commissioner hated opera and would not be at all upset at being delayed and missing the start of the production.

"Two children came to the police station at Rue Dante early yesterday morning claiming we had taken their mother from them. They were booked into the system, which is why I now need you here as witnesses. Or rather, I need you to quell any questions that might arise beyond this night," Inspector Monde explained.

The Commissioner nodded while the Cardinal looked puzzled.

"Why did you need the Cardinal?" the Chief Inspector asked. "Would we not be enough?"

"The children were sent to the nuns at Our Blessed Mary's Orphanage. You know how upset they get when children go missing."

The Chief Inspector nodded his understanding.

"Am I missing something?" the Cardinal asked. "Surely we do not mean to do harm to these children?"

"Quite the contrary," Monde said quietly. "I hope to right a wrong and to prevent them from doing any harm to us."

The Cardinal was obviously not satisfied with Monde's answer, but before he could ask further questions there was a knock at the door.

"The nuns of Blessed Mary do like to be early for their appointments," the Chief Inspector said with a slight grin on his face. He sobered instantly as the knock came again.

Jean-Paul went to the morgue doors and opened one of them a crack. He then opened it fully to let in an angry looking nun.

"I have left the children waiting in the street outside. How can you ask me to bring them to a morgue in the dead of night? I will not have it, do you hear?" the nun's words snapped out like gunfire. She was in her late fifties and a very thin woman, but if anger counted as a measure, you would regard her as being in the heavyweight class. Her eyes roved the room until she spotted the Cardinal. Then she crossed herself in shock as she recognised him.

The doors to the room were forced open as if they had been hit by a hurricane. Jean-Paul who was standing closest to them was flung across the room, sliding to a halt in front of Inspector Monde. The Inspector helped him up as the two children burst into the room.

Anne-Laure Charbonneau entered first. She walked in quietly enough but her eyes glowed red in the gloom, and there was no mistaking the power she carried inside her.

"Have you found her, Inspector?" she asked in a voice so unlike that of a child, being more reminiscent of an angry teacher.

"We are tired of being patient," her brother said as he entered the room. He made a sweeping gesture with his hand and the nun, Cardinal, Chief, Commissionaire and Bernache were thrust away into the far corner. Since Bernache was already most of the way there, everybody else slammed into him.

"I have found your mother," Inspector Monde said and swung his arms in a gesture, pointing the children towards the furthest marble slab, which was covered in a thin white sheet.

Anne-Laure strode to the slab and pulled the sheet away, revealing a burnt and blackened skeleton. The skeleton's skull was turned towards her, its disconnected jaw grinning slackly.

"Oh dear Mama, I see you are well. We have missed you so," the girl said, her voice becoming tender for the first time in the Inspector's hearing.

The skeleton slowly covered itself in sinew and flesh. At first, the flesh was burnt and blackened but it reddened as they watched. In the corner, the nun fainted away into the arms of the Cardinal, whose face turned as white as snow. Bernache ejaculated 'Sacre Bleu' as was his want in these situations.

The flesh on the skeleton healed in front of them until a young woman lay on the slab. She grew clothes in much the same way she had grown flesh.

"Anne-Laure, Pierre-Louis, I thought I had lost you both. How dare you go wandering off without me?" the woman told her two children. She got off the slab leaving the skeleton still visible behind her.

"We did not, Mama," Anne-Laure replied indignantly. "You were taken by men, so we went to the police station to get you back. The Inspector has found you for us."

"Mademoiselle Charbonneau, if I might explain?" Inspector Monde asked. He walked over to the woman, took her hand in his and kissed it lightly. "You and your children were separated when builders cleared the site where you have been residing. As you can see, you are now together again."

The Inspector removed the white sheets on the other two slabs revealing the blackened bones of the two children. Marie-Amable Charbonneau walked over to the bones and caressed the skull of her son with her delicate long pale fingers.

"What do you plan to do with us now, Inspector?" she asked him.

"Would burial in consecrated ground suit you?"

Marie-Amable Charbonneau smiled at the Inspector. "That would suit us very well indeed, Inspector. We have not been able to rest where we were. It was all so bleak and unpleasant."

"I shall make sure you get a grave near flowers, roses if you would like?"

"That would be most suitable." Marie-Amable turned to her children. "Come on children. It is time you went to sleep." She picked each child up in turn and put them on the appropriate slab. Anne-Laure looked a little angry at this treatment, but when her mother kissed her, she slipped over her skeleton and disappeared.

"Do not disappoint me, Inspector. That would not be a sensible thing to do," Marie-Amable warned as she settled back on her own slab and vanished.

"As always Inspector, you do not fail to deliver," the Commissioner de Police said as he walked over to look closer at the skeletons on the slabs. "But perhaps next time, you could arrange for the ghosts to arrive a little later in the evening. As it is, I am only going to miss the first act."

"If you have any problems finding a suitable grave, contact me," the Cardinal said from beside the door. He was away down the corridor within a second of finishing his speech.

"I think you have made a believer of the Cardinal," Jean-Paul told his friend dryly. "It was worth getting a bruised shoulder just for that, Charles."

The Chief Inspector went over and patted Monde gently on the shoulder before leaving the room. The nun came over to Monde and glared straight into his face from as close as she could get.

"If you find any more ghost children on the street, can I recommend you take them to the Sisters of Mercy? They run a fine orphanage, I am told."

"And deny them your milk of human kindness," Inspector Monde said as she walked from the room. "How could I possibly do that?"

Jean-Paul suppressed a giggle. "You go too far sometimes, Charles. But I do admire you."

Bernache walked up to the Inspector. "If I may, I will go now sir. For some reason I feel the need to visit a church and pray."

Inspector Monde had the family buried together beside a beautiful little church in a single grave, the mother below, her children just inches above.

Engraved on the gravestone were their names and the words that the Inspector thought most appropriate:

'May they rest here in peace, bound together in love.'

The End

The Lost Girls

I

Paris in the winter can be a magical town. Falling snowflakes reflect the lights on the Eiffel Tower as night falls. It is one of the most elegant of cities in the world.

It is the winter of nineteen sixty and not everything is wonderful in Paris. Gangs of youths can be found if you look closely enough. The beat generation is growing up, dissolute and wanting to find something better than the world their parents have created. For them, the war is a distant memory and they feel there has to be something more to life than hard work. They experiment with drugs and sex, in much the same way as the youth of the nineteen thirties did.

There are a few streets in Paris that you wouldn't walk down alone, on any night. Places where the Moroccan immigrants live, for example. Young people, more willing to use a knife on someone than the native-born Frenchman would, stalk its streets.

There are the young who shun their parents' world and have their own places. Beat Café's where young poets recite verse that would shock their parents with the crudity of its language, places where jazz is played in the raw. Where young girls go to experience real life, and young men go to have sex with them before they realise that only pregnancy is real in the end.

Like in any large city, teenagers go missing in Paris. They get lost, get drunk, or just choose to run away. A few are found as flotsam on the banks of the Seine, gutted in a fight or pushed to suicide at what they have become. Where some of them end up, no one knows.

There are many old building in Paris. Large wood and brick mansions, built for a different time when servants were cheap and the rich bore large families. Some have been turned into flats while others become a shadow of what they once were. Like rotting teeth once shining in their brilliance, they now decay decadently, the sweet smell of rot filling their rooms.

In one such house, screams from the cellar go unheeded. Unheard from the street, they are the sobbing cries of a young girl writhing in despair, held fast to the cellar wall by thick iron chains.

The girl screamed while her blood dripped through a plastic tube inserted into her arm with a hollow needle. She was not alone in the cellar. Five other girls sat fastened around the walls, but they watched her silently and were inexplicably calm. Her blood and that of the others slowly filled a large bottle beyond their reach. The drip had been set so that they might replenish their blood as they sat. The screamer would eventually die from blood loss, as would the other girls, but it would take them a considerable time.

"I cannot believe I am being made to go to this stupid party," Inspector Monde complained bitterly to Louis Bernache. Bernache nodded his head in apparent agreement, although the truth was that he would have done almost anything to be invited to a soirée at the Commissioner de Police's home. However, he knew Inspector Monde was not a man who enjoyed the company of others, especially when the guests were so far removed from what he understood.

"I tried to back out of it as soon as I received the invitation," Inspector Monde continued. "But the Chief Inspector took the time to come down to tell me I must attend. What is the world coming too when an Inspector de Police is forced to attend a party of the rich and famous. Let me tell you, Louis, the sixties are going to be a time of change and much of it will not be for the better. There will be rioting on the street before long."

"Surely not Inspector," Louis said soothingly. "Shouldn't you be getting changed into evening dress? I thought this affair required you to wear formal attire."

"The day I am forced to dress up as a penguin will be the day I quit the force, Louis. I intend to wear my grey coat and hope no one notices." The Inspector appeared to believe that such a thing might actually be possible. "They will be too busy standing around drinking cocktails and eating sea life on the end of little wooden sticks to notice me."

"Do you not think you will be conspicuous in a grey coat when everyone else is dressed in black?" Louis enquired. He had been the Inspector's assistant for longer than any other had managed, and yet the inspector's naiveté on things in normal life continued to astound him. Just as the things he had seen in the cases the Inspector dealt with chilled his blood and gave him nightmares.

"Ah Louis, but I have a plan!" the Inspector said triumphantly. "You are going to come knocking on the Commissioner's door half an hour after I enter and say I am needed urgently. I will tell the staff that I'll give them my coat when I have warmed up from the night, and then I'll be called away. It is a brilliant plan is it not, mon ami?"

"If you say so Inspector," Bernache replied, suppressing a sigh. Inspector Monde was convinced that Bernache's social life was as limited as his own. Bernache had arranged to meet a very attractive young lady for a meal in an expensive restaurant.

"You will come with me now. We shall share a cab and you can wait in it until half an hour has passed. Then you will come and get me from the party and we can use the cab to get back into the city."

"Sir, would it be possible for me to take the cab, after I rescue you?"

The Inspector grinned at his assistant. "Is she very attractive?"

"Not only attractive sir, but willing, if the restaurant serves its usual fare."

"Will you be late for her if you come with me?" the Inspector asked. Bernache shook his head but Monde read the answer in his eyes.

"You need not bother coming. I shall find another excuse to leave."

"But sir," Bernache replied, though his protest sounded hollow in his ears.

"It is decided. I shall go alone. Have a good evening with your young lady. Remember that in Paris, a gentleman always comes last, as a lady's satisfaction must be guaranteed."

Bernache blushed at the Inspector's joke. He turned his head away in embarrassment, and when he looked up again he discovered the Inspector was gone. Bernache smiled in appreciation, the Inspector truly was a good man, regardless of the dark paths he trod.

33

The Commissioner's butler was most offended by Inspector Monde's refusal to part with his coat, affronted by the very suggestion that the ballroom was not at the perfect temperature for the Commissioner's guests. However, like many men before him, he discovered that in a battle of wills the Inspector always won.

Inspector Monde took a glass of champagne from a maid's loaded tray. He noted in passing how pretty the girl was and how her uniform hugged provocatively tight at her chest and across her derriere.

Without Bernache coming to provide an excuse, Monde decided his best exit strategy was to claim a severe migraine at the first opportunity. It was therefore necessary to find and greet the Commissioner and the Chief Inspector as soon as possible, so they would recognise that he had been here in the first place.

To Monde's considerable surprise, it was the Commissioner who sought him out, arriving behind Monde with an extremely well dressed couple in tow.

"Ah Charles, how good to see you again," the Commissioner said jovially. "I know this is not your kind of affair but I had to bring you and the Bélanger's together somewhere where you could talk in private."

"Is this a matter of urgency?" Inspector Monde had heard of Maurice Bélanger and recognised him at once. He was an important financier with contacts in the government. Madame Bélanger looked at Monde as if she was ready to burst into tears at any moment, but he could also see hope in her eyes.

"You must find our little Doriane for us, Monsieur Inspector," Madame Bélanger begged him. "We are so worried about her."

They made their way separately to a private office off the ballroom so no one would suspect they were together for that purpose. The Bélanger's went first, and once they had been there for a few minutes, Inspector Monde followed. The Commissioner de Police left them to talk as he went off to be the perfect host among his other party guests.

"Perhaps you can tell me the problem?" Inspector Monde asked Maurice.

Madame Bélanger moved forward and thrust a photograph into the Inspector's hands. A surly looking young female stared back at him. She was dressed in a too tight black pullover and short black skirt over tights. She was wearing a beret at a jaunty angle, but on the girl, it looked like an act of defiance.

"This, I take it, is Doriane?" the Inspector asked

"She is fifteen. She has been missing for seven weeks now," Maurice explained. "She is our daughter," he stated unnecessarily.

"And you have already informed the police?"

"Non, she might be kidnapped if the people with her know who she is. I have no wish to subject my daughter or myself to such an ordeal."

"So, she was not kidnapped in the first place?"

"Our daughter can be very wilful," Madame Bélanger explained apologetically. "She has run away from us before, when she does not get her own way. My husband, Maurice, decided to send her to an exclusive Finishing School in Switzerland and she did not want to be parted from her friends."

"It would have been good for her," Maurice said defiantly.

"They are very strict there, Maurice. They physically punish girls who break their rules," Madame Bélanger chided her husband. "But that does not matter now. All we want is for our daughter to be returned safely and discreetly, Inspector. The Commissioner has assured us you can be discreet."

"Have you a list of her friends?" Inspector Monde asked.

Madame Bélanger blushed in embarrassment. "I'm afraid we don't Inspector. Doriane has been a bit of a wild child for some time. We know she attends beat cafés along the banks of the Seine if that is of any help?"

"It will have to do," Inspector Monde replied, putting the girl's photo in his pocket. "I shall begin investigating at once, if that is all right with you?"

The couple nodded and the Inspector walked out of the room and headed for the front door.

"Do you think he will find her?" Madame Bélanger asked her husband as she put her arm around him.

"If she is still alive, and perhaps even if she isn't," her husband replied stone-faced.

II

The snow on the ground had turned to ice making walking dangerous on the streets. It was approaching midnight and Inspector Monde was rapidly running out of contacts he could ask about the missing girl. He walked down a side street towards the Blue Emerald. The Blue Emerald was a club where jazz played and where an underage girl would be made welcome, provided she was pretty.

A blue neon light in the shape of a diamond flashed on and off at the end of an alleyway, which was otherwise unlit. Monde cursed as his right foot slid sideways on the invisible ice.

"I did not know the police were allowed to swear, or that Inspectors of the police even knew such words," a familiar young voice said from the darkness. A shadow detached itself from the wall and became a foreign looking young man in a thick fur coat and similar hat.

"You look like a Cossack, Rico. The last time I saw you, you were pretending to be from Mexico," Inspector Monde replied. Rico lit two cigarettes and handed one to the Inspector. By the light of the match, Monde saw that Rico's features looked pale and drawn.

"That was in the early chill of autumn, when a young girl's fancy turns to thoughts of being kept warm by a man, inside and out. The fur coat has a similar effect on them now the weather is freezing and their fashionable short coats fail to keep their thighs warm."

"Do you ever think of anything but sex, Rico?" Inspector Monde asked. He shook his head at Rico's words. Despite this, the Inspector smiled, for he knew Rico had a good heart, even if he was incorrigible.

"You wrong me, Inspector," Rico said putting his hands to his chest as if mortally wounded. "I'm also very fond of wine and a well prepared Steak Diane. Besides, it is the girls who fondle me, pushing their moist little bodies against me. I'm only human after all. It's not my fault if I rise to their demands."

The Inspector put a hand on Rico's shoulder and guided him out of the alley. "I have some questions to ask you. There is a café down the road where I can buy you an espresso. You look like you could use one."

The café in question was the Midnight Café. It was run by a bald fat man called Emile Fornier and Inspector Monde had not been in it for many months. From the scowl on Fornier's face as he entered, those months had not been long enough.

"As if trade was not bad enough, the mad Inspector de Police comes to drive my remaining custom away," Fornier grumbled as Monde approached.

Monde turned and looked pointedly around the café. He and Rico were Fornier's only customers.

"I cannot drive away what isn't there, unless you are serving ghosts again?"

"Can I get the Inspector something?" Fornier asked sarcastically, ignoring the question.

"Two espressos and a much better attitude, Emile. I might remind you I have some influence with those people who licence the cafés in this town."

"You would be doing me a favour," Fornier mumbled under his breath as he prepared the drinks. Monde led Rico to a table and sat down.

"I am looking for a girl, Rico," The Inspector explained after they had taken sips from their coffees. "A missing girl, I should explain. I am sure you could procure the other kind with a snap of your fingers."

Rico leaned closer to the Inspector. "I am looking also, Inspector. In my case, it is my cousin, Gabriel. She's sixteen and has been missing for nearly two weeks. Her mother is frantic with worry and I promised I would help, but I cannot find a trace of her."

"That is an interesting coincidence."

"Not really, over the last two months at least four girls have gone missing from the streets," Rico said wearily. "When you go around asking enough questions you discover things."

"None of them have been reported to the police," Monde pointed out. He had checked on that very fact shortly after leaving the Commissioner's party.

37

"These are not the sort of girls that are reported missing. They are girls who have run away from home, who have been working as prostitutes, who will not be missed."

"Like your cousin?"

"Yes, like my cousin," Rico said sadly, peering into his cup. "She is a user, an expensive habit that must be paid for somehow."

"Are there any other characteristics they share?"

"They are all between fifteen and seventeen and very pretty. Tell me about your missing girl, Inspector, perhaps I have already come across her."

Monde handed over the photograph to Rico.

"Joan d'Arc," Rico said in surprise as he looked at the photo.

"I don't think so," Inspector Monde responded, "She is by no means a saint and her name is Doriane."

"Quite possibly, but young people do not always use their real names in clubs. I know this girl and she calls herself Joan d'Arc. I saw her only last week in the Blue Emerald. She was with a woman I do not like at all."

"I thought you liked all women, Rico."

"Not this one, there is something weird about her. She is quite good looking, in her thirties, I would guess. She dresses as though she was living fifty years ago, and always in black. We call her the black widow, but never to her face. Her name is Isabella, though Isabella what, I do not know. She started turning up at the Blue Emerald in the autumn, though I know she goes to another club as well. And that is another reason to avoid her."

Inspector Monde raised his eyebrows questioningly and waited for the youth to explain.

"There is a private, very exclusive club not far from here. It opens after midnight and closes at four in the morning. It is called the Black Moon and she is a member of it."

"I thought I knew all the clubs in this part of Paris, but I've never heard of it," the Inspector confessed.

"You can only get in if you have a membership card. The card is jet black on both sides. I have tried to fake the card and the doorman saw through it instantly," Rico explained soberly. "I cannot explain why, but there is something wrong about that woman and her club."

Inspector Monde checked his watch. It was quarter to midnight. "Take me to this club. If you point out this woman to me as she enters, I can trail her back to her apartment and discover if Doriane is there."

Rico shrugged and both men stood up. As they walked out of the café, Inspector Monde heard Emile Fornier whisper 'Good riddance'. The café owner lacked even a modicum of common sense, it seemed.

The Black Moon was ten minutes' walk away. When they got there, Monde was far from convinced it was a club at all. They stood in an unlit alleyway. A single low wattage light bulb burned over a solid black door. There were no signs or markings of any kind to indicate the door led anywhere.

The two men huddled in a doorway fifty feet away from the club and waited. Inspector Monde felt the cold of the night seep through his coat and hat. Rico's clothing no longer seemed so eccentric and Monde felt envious.

Two people drifted into the alleyway, their feet making no sound. They lightly knocked on the door. A hatch at eye level opened before quickly slamming shut again. The door opened and the couple entered. "Neither was her," Rico said unnecessarily as Monde was sure the people had been men.

Between midnight and one in the morning another five people knocked at the door and a woman left as they entered. Though three of the people had been women, none was Isabella according to Rico. By two o'clock in the morning, Monde felt he had wasted enough time.

"Go home and get some sleep, Rico. I am going to enter this club and ask a few questions."

"They will not let you in, Inspector," Rico stated bleakly.

"We shall see," the Inspector said. He left the shelter of their doorway and headed over to the club door. Rico waited in the shadows to see what would happen next.

Monde knocked at the door a little more harshly than the club members had done. The hatch slid open and Monde positioned his identity card where the person inside could read it. "Open up," Monde demanded.

The door opened reluctantly and Monde walked in. The club was obviously below ground, as a poorly lit staircase led down into darkness. As Monde walked down the stairs, he saw the doorman put on his coat and leave, closing the door quietly behind him.

When Monde reached the bottom of the stairs, he found he was in a small converted cellar. There were no windows. Along the far side of the cellar were arched alcoves, each with its own table. There was very little light in the room and that was red. The six people Monde had seen enter huddled in pairs at the tables in the alcoves. Each table had a small table lamp on it, equipped with a low wattage red bulb. Dark shades blocked most of the light from the lamps. To Monde's left was a long bar with a man behind it.

As soon as he entered the room, the talking at the tables ceased. Six pairs of eyes locked on his face. Without saying a word, the people stood up and started to put their coats on. By the time he reached the black marble bar, the club's members were on their way to the stairs. Monde rested his back against the bar and watched them leave.

"You certainly know how to clear a room, Inspector," the man standing behind the bar said without a trace of irony. If anything, he sounded impressed.

"I do not remember telling you my occupation or rank," The Inspector said as he turned to look closely at the man speaking to him. "Your doorman left without telling you anything."

"You are the famous Inspector Charles Monde of the Prefecture De Police," the man replied with a smile. "I have known who you were since the day I arrived in Paris. My name is Cervantes and I am the owner of the Black Moon."

"I am hardly famous," the Inspector pointed out. "My name is rarely, if ever, in the papers as I work hard to keep it out of them."

"But in certain circles your name is legend," Cervantes replied. "I had been hoping to keep this club away from your interest for longer than this."

Cervantes was a tall, very thin man. He dressed in black, making it difficult to see him clearly in the limited light of the room. The red lighting reflected in his eyes, giving them a sinister glow.

"Would you like a drink, Inspector? I doubt your tastes are the same as mine but I have a red wine you might like to sample."

"Why not?" the Inspector replied.

It was at this point the Inspector noticed the glasses behind the bar were made of dark red glass. He had thought their colour was a trick of the light until two glasses were placed on the bar in front of him. Cervantes pulled the cork on a dusty bottle of wine he took from under the bar and poured wine into both glasses. The red wine looked black inside the glasses and the Inspector found that it reminded him chillingly of blood.

"Chin, chin," Cervantes said in salute as he took a sip from his glass. The man shuddered as if wine was not something he usually drank.

"I am looking for Isabella. I believe she may be harbouring a child who needs to be returned to her parents," the Inspector remarked. He decided not to taste the wine and carefully put the glass back on the bar.

"We have rules in this club, Inspector. Rules to keep you away in part. Isabella would not have taken a child."

"Do club members never break the rules?"

"Not twice, once they are found out," Cervantes remarked lightly. The Inspector found himself shivering at his words.

"Isabella's address?"

"I will write it down for you," Cervantes said. He took a sheet of thick paper from beneath the bar, followed by an old fashioned sharpened quill pen.

"I seem to have misplaced my ink pot," Cervantes said quietly. "No matter, I will make do."

Cervantes drew the sharpened tip of the quill across his left thumb, causing a small amount of blood to trickle down it. He used his blood as ink, scratching the address across the paper.

"Thank you," Monde said quietly as the wet paper was handed over to him. He held it carefully by the edge and waved it so the blood would dry quickly.

"Thank you Inspector. It is a rare privilege to meet a legend and to discover he lives up to his reputation." Cervantes gave the Inspector a small bow.

Inspector Monde walked up the stairs slowly and carefully to avoid falling in the poor light. All the way to the outside door, he could feel an itch across his shoulder blades and the urge to run from the club was almost irresistible, but he would not give Cervantes the satisfaction. He had never before felt as much relief as he did when he finally pushed the club door closed behind him and leant on it, breathing heavily.

III

As Inspector Monde walked out of the alleyway, a heavy hand fell on his shoulder and he turned in fright, ready to fight for his life. Rico backed away, his hands raised in surrender at the Inspector's reaction.

"I give in, Monsieur Inspector. I was waiting for you back in the doorway."

"That was most foolish of you, Rico," the Inspector replied while hoping his heart was not going to explode, given the pace it was currently beating. "But since you are here, you can tell me what you know about this address."

The Inspector drew out the piece of paper Cervantes had given him from his coat and handed it over. Rico turned it so that the light from a street lamp fell onto its surface.

"This paper is vellum, Inspector, made from animal hide. My father restored old books when I was a child and I recognise it. The ink is unusual too," Rico said, squinting at the sheet in the poor light.

"It is written in blood. Ignore that, what do you know of the address?"

Rico almost dropped the sheet of paper. He handed it back to Monde in much the same way Monde had handled it, touching only the edges. Monde put it back carefully in his pocket.

"There are many grand old houses in that part of the city, falling apart now as so many of their owners suffered financially during the war."

"You do not recognise the address though?"

"No, I've never been to that house. Is it where Isabella lives?"

"So I have been told, Rico. I shall investigate it in the morning." The Inspector turned the collar of his coat up. "When I have found the Doriane girl, I shall help you look for your cousin."

"I hoped that finding her would not require your kind of help, Inspector," Rico said and turned to head in the opposite direction. "Good hunting, Inspector."

Winter is usually kind on the appearance of old houses. The cold stops any smell of wood rot and a soft layer of white snow hides many imperfections. Despite that, to Inspector Monde, the house that the piece of paper indicated reeked of decay.

He had watched it closely for half an hour and seen no signs of movement inside it. The roof was covered in snow, which suggested the house was cold and no fires burned within it. Certainly, there was no hint of smoke from any of its four chimneys. All the curtains in the windows Monde could see were drawn shut. Only the driveway leading up to the front door gave any hint of occupancy. Footprints going both in and out of the house had compressed the otherwise pristine snow into ice.

The morning sky was overcast. The snow made the scene look like something out of a picture postcard. All it needed to complete it were robins in the foreground.

Monde waited until eleven o'clock before he decided to enter the house. Strictly against police custom and practice, he intended to break in rather than knock at the door. He had mulled over the events of the night before and reached certain worrying conclusions.

Inspector Monde walked carefully up the drive, trying to place his own boots on existing footprints so it would be difficult to spot he had been there. The front door looked impregnable, built in an age when the rich took some precautions to protect themselves against the local thieves. Monde looked at the door and took a gamble. He grasped and turned its handle. It was unlocked. The door opened silently on recently oiled hinges.

There was a smell of damp in the house, along with another smell that Monde couldn't identify except that it was sweet and cloying. He stepped lightly into the hallway and shut the door behind him. The scream for help he heard was muffled but unmistakable.

Monde wondered how anybody could possible know he had entered the house. The scream for help rang out another two times before the voice drifted away to silence in despair. Monde realised this was someone screaming at random and not in response to anything the person had heard.

Most men would have called out in response to the cry for help, but Monde was not a typical man. The cry appeared to be coming from below. Monde stepped quietly and carefully through the house looking to find a door leading to the cellar. He finally found it in the kitchen and crept down winding stone steps to the cellar. It was too dark to see, so the Inspector took out the torch he had brought in his pocket and switched it on. The beam cut brightly through the darkness.

The sweet smell he first detected grew stronger as he descended and was mixed with that of urine and worse. He recognised the smell as that of decaying flesh. When he reached the bottom of the steps, he ran the beam away from his feet and across to the walls.

"Mon dieu!" he gasped in horror. The room was laid out like a medieval dungeon. Young girls were chained to the walls. From each of their arms a rubber tube ran towards a large wine making bottle on the floor. The bottle was nearly full of blood.

The girls sat on a stone bench that ran along the side of the wall. The chains shackled their arms in the air while their feet were chained to the wall. All the girls looked to be dead, their heads lolling onto their chests.

"Help me!" a girl's voice called from the other side of the room. Inspector Monde swung his torch straight into the eyes of a girl on the opposite wall. He recognised her instantly as Doriane. "Move the light away, you're blinding me!" she complained, swinging her head in an effort to get out of its beam.

"Sorry." Inspector Monde pointed the torch to shine at the floor and hurried over to her. He took one look at the pipe in her arm and pulled it out. Doriane muffled a scream. The Inspector pulled a clean handkerchief from his pocket and tied it round her arm to staunch the bleeding.

"How long have you been here?" he asked as he examined the shackles binding her. He would need a bolt cutter to free her.

"About a week, I think. I ran out of money and Isabella said I could stay at her place. The next thing I knew I was down here. My name is Joan and I need you to help me escape."

"Your name is Doriane and your parents are frantic with worry."

"Shush. Not in front of the other girls. I don't want them to know who I am." Doriane whispered, furious at the Inspector for giving her name away.

"The other girls have been dead for days if not weeks," Monde told her glumly.

"That's nonsense," Doriane replied. "They sleep for a long time because they are exhausted, but I had a long conversation with them only a few hours ago. One of the girls told me her name was Gabriel and that her family was sure to be searching for her."

Inspector Monde felt a chill run through him as a grim possibility occurred to him. He left Doriane's side and walked over to the first girl on the other wall. He lifted her head and shone the torch on her face. She was certainly dead, but that was not all she was. Grimly he examined each girl in turn and found the same thing.

"Doriane, I have to go and fetch some tools to set you free. Can you wait here a little longer in the dark?"

"Isabella may come. She brings water and food to us. She last came a few hours ago. The girls can't be dead, they told her how they were ready to serve her and she should let them loose." Doriane paused. "It's not their fault they sounded a little crazy. It's what being imprisoned does to you."

"Isabella will not come for a few hours," the Inspector said as he consulted his watch. It was already midday. He had a lot to do and very little time left to do it. "I understand about your friends and nobody would blame them for what has become of them. I have to go now. I will be back soon."

"Are you going to bring the police?" Doriane asked.

"I am the police. My name is Inspector Charles Monde. Rest assured I will end this situation in the best traditions of France."

Inspector Monde went over to Doriane and kissed her lightly on the forehead. "I know this is hard on you, but I must ask you to be strong. I will not be away long."

It was three o'clock in the afternoon by the time Inspector Monde collected together most of the equipment he needed. He drove through the streets of Paris in a daze heading for the Church of Saint-Gervais. He was running out of time. However, he needed to visit one last place before he could go back to Doriane.

The Church of Saint-Gervais was built in the fourth century and lay in the oldest parish in Paris on the right bank of the Seine. It had been rebuilt many times over the century and the current church was a triumph of gothic architecture. For Inspector Monde it was exactly the right church to visit, and not only because he knew Father Dubois who was its senior priest.

"We do not usually allow people to fill their hip flasks with holy water," a stern voice told Inspector Monde. Monde turned around, startled to see Father Dubois glaring at him. He smiled back in return.

"Forgive me father, but what I am doing, I am doing as the Lord's work."

"I have just had two nuns and a young priest rush me out of my office to deal with the madman draining holy water from a font. I should not be surprised to find that the culprit is you, Charles."

The Inspector opened his mouth to explain but Father Dubois held up a hand to silence him.

"I feel that my nights will be clearer of nightmares if you would do me the courtesy of not telling me what you are up to. Just take the water and go, Charles."

"A blessing for what I am about to do would not come amiss in the circumstances," the Inspector said quietly.

"Provided you go to Notre Dame or some other church to take confession later. Please stay away from here. One of my priests was traumatised for weeks after you told him the story of Marie."

"This is my parish church, Father."

"Nevertheless..." Father Dubois said firmly. When Inspector Monde nodded his agreement, the priest placed a quick blessing on him. His hip flask had filled itself while in the font and Monde retrieved it, carefully wiping it dry.

"Good luck my friend..." Father Dubois whispered as Inspector Monde left the church.

When Inspector Monde got back to his car, he found Rico standing beside it.

"It occurred to me this morning that it was highly unlikely we had two people in Paris kidnapping young girls," Rico said, by way of introduction. "And all these disappearances started after this woman Isabella came to Paris. I've been looking for you and I want to come with you."

"Believe me, Rico, when I say that if you knew what I know, the last place you would want to be is with me in the next hour," Inspector Monde said soberly.

"She is my cousin..."

"Very well, get in the car, but do not interfere with me, whatever you see," the Inspector snapped. At this time of the year, the sun would set by four in the afternoon and the Inspector had little time left.

The house looked unchanged since the morning. Monde led Rico into the house, making him carry the large carpetbag the Inspector had in the boot of his car.

"What's in this thing?" Rico asked as they walked up the drive, "It weighs a ton."

"Try and be quiet Rico," the Inspector whispered. "The life you save by doing so may be your own."

"Jesus and Mary in Heaven!" Rico exclaimed as he saw the girls in the cellar. "Is Gabriel among them?"

The Inspector shrugged and allowed Rico to look for her as he opened the carpetbag and retrieved a wooden stake along with a heavy lump hammer.

"What are you doing?" Doriane screamed from the other side of the room. She had been in a doze until the men had woken her.

"You cannot be serious," Rico exclaimed as Monde placed the stake against the chest of the girl nearest him. "This one is Gabriel," he said touching gently the back of the head of the furthest away of the girls. "I need to take her body back to her mother. Her death is going to be difficult enough to explain without having to explain why some idiot policeman desecrated her body after death."

"Watch and learn," the Inspector said through narrowed lips and hit the end of the stake hard with the lump hammer. The dead girl sat bolt upright and screamed. The hammer swung again and her heart was pierced. She gasped, smiled for a second at the Inspector and then dissolved into dust.

Doriane began screaming, only stopping to gulp down more air into her lungs before starting again. The Inspector moved to the second chained girl and repeated the grisly task.

When he reached the body of Gabriel, Rico placed a warning hand on his shoulder. Monde looked up at him. "Would you rather she remained a creature of the night, her soul tormented in hell?"

Rico paused to think and then removed his hand. Inspector Monde released Gabriel from her fate.

The two men moved over to Doriane who had stopped screaming and was sobbing quietly. She looked up at the Inspector with wide round eyes. "Is it my turn to die, Inspector?"

The Inspector shook his head, "I do not know. Will you drink some water for me?"

Doriane nodded her head and the Inspector took out his hip flask and offered her a drink. He held it to her lips as she gratefully drank it all down. When it was all gone, she smiled at him. "Thank you."

"Cut her loose Rico. There are bolt cutters in the bag."

Rico cut her free and the two men helped Doriane up the steps to freedom. She was far too weak from her ordeal to walk on her own. When they got to the front door, Monde freed himself from Doriane and looked at Rico.

"Take her some way from the house. I intend to burn it to the ground."

"What about Isabella?" Rico asked.

"Her too, if I can get this done before the sun sets."

There was a can of petrol in the carpetbag and Monde spilled fuel over the floors and walls of the house, paying particular attention to the stairs to the upper floor. He then walked to the front door and lit a match, throwing it into the house and closing the door behind him. The light of flames lit his back as he walked down the path to where Rico and Doriane were waiting.

The house burned fiercely as the three watched. Nothing living or dead could survive such an intense conflagration.

"You lied," Doriane told the Inspector as she watched the house burn.

"About what?" the Inspector asked.

"That flask, it contained whisky or brandy or something like that. It has been burning in my tummy ever since I drank it."

"I am truly sorry," Monde said with deep regret in his voice. "It was holy water."

Doriane burped and a blue flame shot from her lips. She looked at Inspector Monde with horror as she realised the truth. Then she smiled.

"Tell my mother I love her," she said simply. Flames shot from her mouth, she fell to the ground and lay still.

Rico turned her over so she was looking up at them with blue dead eyes. Her lips were black, burnt by the fire within that had killed her. She looked like an angel in death.

Inspector Monde was lighting votive candles in the Church of Saint-Gervais. He had just lit the sixth and last when he heard someone behind him. He turned to see Father Dubois.

"Six is a lot of people to remember at one time." Father Dubois remarked.

"Six young girls, all now in heaven," Inspector Monde replied enigmatically.

"And what of your wife, may I ask?"

"I pray she is there to greet them."

The End

Bloody Hands

I

Of all the places to see in the spring, Paris should be the top of the list for everyone who loves the splendor of old imperial cities. The parks bloom with crocuses and daffodils and there is an eagerness for life that is almost palpable.

When frogs spawn and flowers bloom, it is time for the people to put on their brightest clothes and parade down the boulevards for no other reason than to celebrate the return of the sun. Awaking from hibernation is not something only animals do.

In Paris, there are trades that shut down for the winter. One such trade is that of the builder. Ask any bricklayer and they will tell you that you cannot build anything in winter. *'The mortar, it will not set, we cannot dry out the rooms in the cold, my spirit level is frozen,'* they will say. Whether imagined or real, construction stops as the nights draw in and only recommences when the sun and warmth returns.

One set of builders had been eagerly awaiting the start of spring all winter. They waited to repair a building set amidst the very heart of the best shopping district in Paris. It is a shop with an impressive reputation for all things millinery, the finest shop for ladies hats in all of Paris.

The owner and founder, Jacques Allard was forced to sell the shop the previous year due to his age and increasing poor health. He promised the new owner to carry on creating new hats for the shop while he is able. Despite spectacular profits over the years, Jacques Allard had let his shop degenerate into a very poor state. Not only was a new roof needed but also the three upper floors had become dilapidated while the shop's cellar has been closed and unused for nearly fifty years.

The new owner, Christian Delmar, had great plans for the shop and for this he needed to create more floor space than Jacques ever wanted. He contracted his builders to open up and renovate the cellar, so that it too could become a shopping floor. In doing so, he ignored Jacques requests to keep the shop exactly as it had been when he had been the owner.

"If there is a key in this building to get into the cellar, I cannot find it," Pierre Leclerc complained to his boss.

"There must be a key somewhere," Basile Langlois said irritably. "Monsieur Allard showed Monsieur Delmar's architect around this building before it was sold."

"Well, then he must still have it," Pierre insisted. He was the foreman of the crew assigned to clean out the cellar and knock down the interior walls. Pierre was a big man with muscles to match, and he flexed them in a gesture of annoyance. It was supposed to be up to his boss to ensure they could get everywhere they needed to.

Basile sighed in annoyance. This job was going to be trouble. He knew that before the ink dried on the contract. The architect had redesigned the place based on old drawings rather than measuring and there were bound to be differences, there always were. Now he discovered he couldn't even get his men working. Start from the bottom and work up was Basile's motto and that meant clearing the cellar first.

"Should we start clearing the ground floor?" Pierre asked. His work crew were getting irritated as they were paid by results. There were lots of jobs for casual laborers in the spring and if he didn't get things started, he wouldn't be left with any men to manage.

"No, smash the door down," Basile said after considering the situation.

"It says on the plans that this door is to be saved and refurbished," Pierre pointed out.

"There are lots of doors to be thrown away. We will swap this one with one of those." Pierre stood without responding, just long enough to annoy Basile. "Well, get on with it, man. Your men are eager to start work."

The men in question were huddled in a group a short distance away listening to the management's conversation. Some threw their cigarettes to the floor and squashed them out as they realized they were soon to begin work. Paul, a sallow-faced young man, passed a sledgehammer to Pierre, who hefted it experimentally.

51

Pierre knew it was necessary to get the feel of a hammer before you struck it hard against something.

He swung the hammer back and brought it across to smash into the lock of the stout oak door. There was amusement from the men when nothing happened except that the door's handle broke. Whispered bets were placed as Pierre's face reddened under his boss's skeptical gaze.

The second blow pushed the door through its frame. Hinges popped out as the door fell inwards and slid down the stairs beyond. A ragged cheer went up from the men who had bet on the second blow.

For a few seconds there was silence and then a wind rushed up the stairs, throwing Pierre and Basile back. The wind stopped as suddenly as it started.

"What in Mary's name was that?" Pierre asked as several of the men crossed themselves.

"Probably just a door open somewhere," Basile said and shrugged. "I do not care in any case. Get down there and start cleaning it out." No one moved. "If any of you want to get paid today, that is!"

Louis Bernache considered his face carefully in the mirror. He was seriously considering getting rid of the small moustache he had worn since he was old enough to shave. Most gendarmes wore moustaches in the Paris police force, but it was spring and change was in the air. He was wondering how Eve, his girlfriend would react to its removal. She kept saying it tickled, especially when he kissed her intimately, and he was not sure whether this was a good or bad thing.

"Is there a problem with your face?" Inspector Monde asked. Bernache was admiring himself in the men's cloakroom and the Inspector had snuck up behind him.

"Do you think I should shave off my moustache, Inspector?" Bernache enquired.

"Only if your girlfriend requests it," the Inspector replied, showing his usual uncanny gift for getting to the nub of the problem. "You must have little work to do if you can afford to waste your time thinking about such things."

"It has been very quiet recently, Inspector, hasn't it?"

52

"It is the lull before the storm, Louis. I can feel it in my bones. Something powerful is coming, mark my words."

Pierre looked at the architect's plans with annoyance. Somewhere in this room, they had lost four metres. The plans must be wrong. Now that they had nearly cleared the room they could measure the position of the walls, and the width of the building was out by three point seven five metres. His crew stopped work for a cigarette break while he and Paul carried out the measurements.

The boy stopped scratching for a few seconds. He banged his hands hard against the unyielding wood. His fingers bled, their nails ripped to pieces. Nevertheless, he planned to scrape his way through to freedom if he could.

Pierre heard banging from somewhere in the cellar. His crew looked around to see who was doing it and it soon became clear it wasn't any of them.

"It seems to be coming from behind the wall," Paul said. Pierre went to listen, putting his ear against the wall while his men formed a semicircle around him.

"I think I can hear someone sobbing," Pierre told his crew. "Is somebody there?" he shouted as loudly as he could.

The banging stopped. "Hello!" Pierre shouted, but when he pressed his ear against the wall, he could hear nothing.

He turned to his men. "It must be someone in the shop next door."

His crew swore, mouths fell open and cigarettes fell off unresisting lips to tumble to the floor. The men at the back panicked and rushed for the stairs, followed closely in stumbling fashion by the rest of the crew. Several crossed themselves before they ran.

Pierre turned to see what they were looking at.

"Mon Dieu," he said, backing away in horror.

Standing in front of him was a small boy. His eyes were black and hollow. Pierre could see through the child to some extent. The boy held out his hands in appeal to Pierre. His hands dripped with blood as the child's hands were little more than bloody stumps, the finger tips missing and white bone showing through.

Pierre Leclerc considered himself a brave man. However, he was up the stairs and standing by the front door of the shop only a few seconds later.

II

Inspector Monde raised his eyes from the report he was reading as he heard his door open. He was not surprised to see the Chief Inspector approaching. Antoine Tessier was a large man and when he entered a room it appeared to shrink around him. At least, so it seemed to Inspector Monde.

The Chief Inspector took up his usual perch on the edge of Monde's desk. The Inspector wondered, not for the first time, if the Chief worried that the plastic and tubular steel interview chair would not take his weight. All Monde could say for certain was the Chief never tried to sit on it.

"I have a task for you," the Chief said without any preamble.

"Could it have something to do with a certain shop selling hats in the centre of town?" Monde asked.

The Chief looked both astonished and irritated. "How could you know that, Charles? I have asked all the papers to refrain from publishing the story, and there is not a word in them about it."

"I have my own sources of information," the Inspector said, tapping his nose. "I understand the builders involved are now picketing the shop. It seems a very strange way to rid themselves of a ghost."

"We do not use the 'G' word in my presence, Charles. They do not exist."

"Nevertheless, you are about to ask me to go and get rid of one, are you not?"

The Chief Inspector grinned at Monde. "Since they do not exist, it shouldn't take you very long. Christian Delmar is a very influential man. He is the new owner of 'Modiste Allard' and he is anxious to avoid bad publicity. I shall be upset if he gets any. Is that understood, Charles?"

54

"Of course, sir. May I ask exactly why there are builders picketing outside his very fine hat shop?"

"When the builders saw the ... thing that does not exist, they refused to return to work until it had been exorcised from the building. The man in charge of the building work is a Monsieur Basile Langlois, and he chose to make a bad situation worse by firing the men for refusing to work. Now they are picketing to prevent any other builders working on the cellar that they refuse to enter. Such a thing could only happen in France." The Chief Inspector put up his hands in resignation.

"I will do my best to resolve the issue with the thing that does not exist, Chief Inspector. However, I have never proved to be good at industrial relations."

"Just get rid of the damned ghost," the Chief Inspector shouted.

There was a knock at the door and Louis Bernache opened it enough to poke his head around. "Is there a problem, Inspector?" He spotted the Chief Inspector and saluted. "I am sorry, sir. I did not know you were here."

"I am not, Gendarme Bernache, as I am already leaving. Make sure the Inspector does a good job." The Chief Inspector left the office, his face slightly pink with embarrassment.

Bernache entered the office and looked expectantly at Inspector Monde, awaiting instructions.

"We have a haunted hat shop mystery to solve Louis. You have heard of 'Modiste Allard', I take it?"

"Eve will buy her hats nowhere else, Inspector, which means that she has not bought a hat in months as the shop has been closed. I never realized how temperamental a woman can get when she cannot satisfy her urge to spend money on clothes." Bernache looked puzzled. "Do you think a woman's brain is wired differently than a man's?"

"I cannot believe a man of your age and experience could ask that question." Inspector Monde smiled. "We must hurry about this task then, if you are to experience peace anytime soon. We will take my car. I'll brief you on the way."

Inspector Monde parked his car a hundred metres down the street when he saw the men gathered about the building. He had just had his car repaired and didn't want it damaged again. There were about a dozen men in the picket and they looked to be in a foul mood.

He approached the men holding his identification in front of him. "Police, official business, get out of the way."

A very large man blocked his path into the building. "My name is Pierre Leclerc and I am the foreman," he said.

"You were there when the apparition appeared?" Monde asked.

"We all were, but I was nearest the *'bloody boy'*."

"The *'bloody boy'*?"

"It is what we've decided to call the poor soul," Pierre explained. "Not that I ever want him near me again, you understand."

"Perhaps you could come inside with us and discuss this?" Monde suggested.

"We are locked out of the building."

Inspector Monde directed Bernache to the front door with an inclination of his head and Bernache walked up to the door and banged imperiously upon it. "Inspector Monde and Gendarme Bernache here to see the owner. Open the door!"

A few seconds later, they heard bolts being drawn. When the door opened, Bernache entered first with Pierre and the Inspector following close behind. As soon as they were in the shop the man who opened the door slammed it closed and bolted it.

"That is hardly necessary. My men are not going to storm the place," Pierre said.

"You should be ashamed of yourself, you traitor," Basile Langlois said furiously as he turned to face them. "You'll never work for me again, Pierre."

"And you are?" the Inspector enquired.

"Basile Langlois, the builder in charge of the work."

"Ah yes, the idiot. Can you take us to Monsieur Delmar? I believe he is currently in the building."

Basile looked affronted at the Inspector's description of him. He contained his frustration and anger and led the group up the stairs to an office on the first floor.

The Inspector looked closely at the people in the room. He had introduced himself to Christian Delmar and asked Pierre to tell them all exactly what he'd seen and heard in the cellar. Basile

56

Langlois snorted derisively at every revelation, and Monde was getting heartily sick of him.

Delmar listened patiently to Pierre and it was not clear to Monde whether he believed the story or not. Christian Delmar seemed to be focused only on getting the work started again.

"I have a suggestion as to a way forward, Inspector," Bernache said when the silence became oppressive. Monde nodded his approval and Bernache continued.

"Why don't we go into the cellar and see if we can get the ghost to appear?"

Basile snorted in disgust. "And how long will we have to wait for such a miracle to happen? I am a busy man."

"Who can achieve nothing while his workers are picketing. No builder in France will cross an official picket line." Monde pointed out.

"Do you think it will help, Inspector?" Delmar enquired.

"What were you doing, before the ghost manifested?" Monde asked.

"We were measuring the distance between the walls. The architect had made a mistake and the walls were nearly four metres closer to each other than it showed on the plans."

"That does not sound like Legrow," Delmar said. "He is a meticulous man. I have used him many times before."

"We shall do that again then," the Inspector suggested. "Pierre and Louis will do the measuring and the rest of us will watch."

Pierre Leclerc gulped. He did not want to show fear before these men, but the truth was he was very afraid.

The cellar was lit by a string of lights the builders had brought with them and these were powered by a petrol generator at the back of the building. The electrical circuits of the shop were off so that there was no risk a workman would cut through a live wire and electrocute himself.

The cellar felt cold and oppressive. Bernache was beginning to regret his idea as he held one end of the measuring tape and called out the measurements to Pierre.

Pierre went to the drawings, which were still lying on the table where he left them from the previous day. "You see," he said with evident satisfaction. "There's nearly a four metre difference from the plan."

"That is impossible," Christian Delmar stated as he bent down to peer more closely at the architect's drawings.

"Some things can be hidden in plain sight," Inspector Monde said enigmatically as he went to the far wall and touched it.

The banging started as soon as his hand touched the wall.

"You see, I told you," Pierre said triumphantly. He had second thoughts and started to back towards the stairs.

"What did you do next?" the Inspector asked sharply.

"I called into the wall, asking if someone needed help."

"Do you need our help?" The Inspector shouted at the wall. "Is there something you want?"

The banging stopped and Inspector Monde looked expectantly at the wall. Then the banging started again, but this time it sounded as if whoever was banging was furious.

The men covered their ears, as the sound became loud enough to deafen them. Dust fell from the cracks between the bricks and the wall began to throb and pulse in time to the banging.

Then a figure came running from out of the wall. A small boy, but with his mouth open unnaturally wide, showing all his teeth. Blood dripped from his mouth and from the stumps of the fingers he held like claws in front of him.

Inspector Monde staggered backwards as the boy ran straight through him, screaming in anger. The lights on the wire exploded one after the other as the boy ran around the room. The last bulb exploded and the cellar fell into darkness.

The boy stopped screaming and the only sounds left in the cellar were the shocked breathing of the men in it. Bernache felt something touching him and wanted to scream. When a hand grasped firmly on to his shoulder, he did.

III

"It is only me, mon amis. Do not panic," Inspector Monde said quietly. Bernache suppressed the second scream he was about to utter and relaxed. The Inspector's calm and unflustered voice was all it took to reduce his fears to nothing.

A match flared in the darkness and the Inspector's face glowed in its light. "Did anybody think to bring a torch?" he asked.

Pierre switched on his torch a few seconds later and swung it around the cellar. "Does anybody still doubt we have a ghost?"

"A very angry ghost if I am not mistaken, Monsieur Leclerc. And is there any wonder under the circumstances?" the Inspector said.

"I will go and get a priest at once," Basile Langlois said in a shaken voice. "I apologise, Pierre. Once we have got rid of this evil I will reinstate your men."

"And pay them for the time they have been standing outside," Pierre suggested hopefully.

Basile hesitated at the thought of paying the men for doing nothing. However, Christian Delmar came to his rescue. "I will pay the men, provided they keep their mouths shut about what they have seen."

"Which is all well and good," Monde said with a sigh. "But a priest is not the answer to this problem. Gendarme Bernache and I have a lot of work to do if we are to put things to rights. I also have a task for Monsieur Leclerc and another of his men, one that will require them to demonstrate a small amount of courage."

The Inspector went over to Pierre and explained exactly what he needed from him.

"And you are sure we will find this thing?" Pierre asked. "More importantly, are you sure we will be safe?"

"If you're doing what the ghost wants, it will be no trouble to you," Monde said confidently.

"I have a worker who trusts me. We will do what you want, Inspector."

"Good," the Inspector said with satisfaction. "Now it is up to Bernache and I to solve the other part of this mystery. Come on, Louis, we have much work to do and it already nearly noon."

Louis Bernache drove the Inspector's car through the heavy Parisian traffic as carefully as he could. No car in Paris spent more than a few weeks of its life without suffering bumps and knocks, but the Inspector always expected his car to arrive in pristine condition.

"Where are we going?" the old man in the back demanded. "I thought we were going to your police station on the Rue Dante?"

Bernache looked at the man through his rear view mirror. He saw a well-preserved distinguished looking man in his eighties. This was Jacques Allard, the most celebrated hat maker in the whole of Paris, the man who had owned the shop for over fifty years. He was a powerful and influential man, which was why Bernache and Inspector Monde spent the day searching the public records office for facts before approaching him.

It was nine in the evening and Paris traffic was making its usual haphazard course through the city, accompanied as always by much blaring of horns and Gallic curses.

"I'm sorry, sir. I told you that Inspector Monde wished to see you urgently on a most important matter and you said you would come. I did not say we would be meeting him at the police station." Bernache explained. In fact, Inspector Monde had told him that under no circumstances should he tell Jacques Allard where he was being taken.

Jacques Allard sat back in his seat grumpily.

Inspector Monde walked down the stairs into the cellar. Two oil lamps burned on the floor and the builders had electric torches clipped to their belts. The wall on the far side had bricks knocked out of it at regular intervals at about eyelevel.

"Have you found it?" Inspector Monde asked them eagerly.

"That we have, Inspector," Paul told him.

"I don't see how you could have known," Pierre said. He wiped the sweat from his brow and leaned on his pickaxe. Whoever built the wall had done a thorough job.

"Start clearing around it. You will need something to open it with," the Inspector instructed.

"Pierre is very good with a sledgehammer," Paul volunteered. "It takes him two blows though."

"Cheeky young whelp," Pierre muttered under his breath.

The Inspector's car drew to a halt directly in front of 'Modiste Allard'. Bernache jumped out and opened the door for Jacques Allard to step out. When Allard realized he was outside the shop that had made him famous, he stopped as if physically struck.

"This shop is my past. I have no wish to visit it again. Take me back home at once."

"Monsieur Allard, you walked into this shop every day for the last fifty years. Surely you are not afraid to go in one last time?" Bernache put a helping hand under Jacques Allard's arm, which was pushed away.

"I am not an invalid, Gendarme. I merely did not want to see my old shop in such a state of disrepair. I already regret selling it to Monsieur Delmar." Jacques stepped up to the doors of the shop as if he was a much younger man and pushed the doors open. Bernache ran to catch up with him.

The ground floor was lit by a string of lights in much the same way as the cellar had been. Jacques Allard went to the stairs to go up to the office.

"Oh no, Monsieur Allard," Bernache said, bringing the old man to a halt. "The Inspector is waiting for you in the cellar."

Jacques Allard's face went white and he nearly fell off the step he stood on. Bernache rushed over to help him but Jacques again pushed him away. Summoning up his strength, Jacques headed unerringly towards the cellar door with Bernache following closely behind.

When Jacques Allard walked down the cellar stairs, he found a table had been set out in the centre of the room with a number of chairs around it. The oil lamps had been positioned so the far wall was in darkness, but it was there that his eyes first looked and they kept darting back to it every few seconds.

"I am sorry to have to bring you here, Monsieur Allard," the Inspector said cheerfully. "However, it is here where things happened and so it is here where we must be."

"I don't know what you are talking about, Inspector. I closed this cellar many decades ago after a dreadful accident. It has painful memories for me."

61

"Come and sit down, and you too, Louis. Sit at the table." The Inspector indicated the two seats on the side of the table facing the far wall. The Inspector sat down facing them, looking calm and relaxed.

Jacques saw shadows move near to the wall. "Who is there, show yourselves!" he shouted. The shadows resolved to become Pierre and Paul as they moved into the light. Paul carried a pickaxe while Pierre held the hammer he used to smash open the door into the cellar.

"They are here with me," the Inspector said dismissively. He waved Jacques and Bernache to sit down. Jacques Allard seemed particularly reluctant to sit down in the cellar.

"You are correct when you said that something terrible happened here. In 1913, your first wife was taking stock out of this very cellar when she fell down the stairs and smashed her skull on the floor. The back of her skull was totally crushed as I understand it."

"It was a terrible, terrible accident," Jacques Allard said with his head downcast.

"But a fortuitous one for all of that," the Inspector continued. "You married for a second time, less than a year after your wife's death, and to a very rich young lady indeed."

"Monique was a wonderful woman. She died last year and her death is part of the reason I sold the shop, Inspector. I lost heart with her gone," Jacques replied, still keeping his eyes downcast.

"And it is certainly true that your business would have failed without her money to bail it out. Bernache and I found records of people taking you to court to pay off your debts in the time leading up to your marriage."

"I loved both my wives, Inspector. My first wife's death was a tragedy."

"And you are very familiar with tragedy, Monsieur Allard, because your son disappeared in the time between the death of your first wife and your marriage to the second. He was what age when he disappeared, ten years old?" The Inspector looked expectantly at Jacques for an answer.

"Nine, he was nine years old when he vanished. I searched everywhere, even put up a large reward, but he was never seen again."

"Well then I have some good news for you Monsieur Allard, for we have certainly found him."

Jacques eyes flicked again to the far wall, confirming the Inspector's suspicions. Inspector Monde picked up one of the two oil lamps and walked to the wall. Bricks and mortar had been pulled away from a section of the wall to reveal a rotted door behind. Black streaks ran down its bottom half.

"The problem with bricking up the door of a room is that some sign of the old door always remains. It takes a certain dedication and time to build a new wall in front of an old one, covering up the door in a way that ensures it cannot be found by mere differences in the colors of the brick or mortar." The Inspector paused as Paul and Pierre cleared the last of the rubble away from the door. "If you were to do this in a shop you would have to do it away from prying eyes, at night perhaps, in a cellar you stopped everyone from going into."

Jacques stood up in alarm as Pierre hefted the hammer in preparation to strike at the door.

"I've never seen that door in my life, Inspector, and have no idea what you're talking about."

"Then you have no need to show alarm, have you, sir? Please sit back down while we work. Pierre, if you please?"

Pierre swung the hammer and the door dropped off its hinges, the wood having rotted away. The door swayed for a second before dropping towards them.

The bottom half of the inside of the door was stained dark black. As the Inspector held the oil lamp closer it became possible to see deep scrape marks. The door had been scratched so deep that in the centre of the scratches the wood had been worn through. What looked like black marks on the outside of the door had actually been holes.

"Such determination," the Inspector said sadly. "Had the door been his only obstacle he would have clawed his way free. Can you imagine what he must have felt like when he found a layer of bricks beyond the door? *Mon Dieu*, it is unthinkable."

Jacques was staring wide eyed beyond the door, into the darkness of the room beyond. He looked as if he planned to bolt for the stairs at any second. Inspector Monde moved the lamp to light the threshold of the room. There were some dusty rags littering the area around the door. The inspector moved one of the rags to reveal the back of the skull of a child, lying where he had fallen. The rags were all that were left of his clothes.

"This is an old building. That room must have been bricked up long before I moved into this shop." Jacques said firmly, though his eyes never shifted from the bones on the floor.

"And everybody who might know different is long dead," the Inspector said and sighed. "You have committed the perfect crime. I cannot prove this child is your son even though we both know it is. We have no fingerprints to match."

"Then I will be leaving," Jacques said and stood up to go. "Thank you for the history lesson, Inspector."

As he turned to leave, the dust in the room stirred as though a breeze ran through it. The breeze became fast enough to stir the clothes of the boy on the floor. Jacques turned to see a skeletal hand with missing finger tops lift from the floor and point at him.

"Don't go, Father," a child's voice said pleadingly. "You locked me in because I saw you hit momma with a shovel. I told you I didn't see, but you still locked me in. I pleaded with you, Poppa, don't lock me in. I screamed for days and I heard you moving outside the door. You never unlocked the door, Papa. Please don't leave me now!"

The skeleton stood up in its rags and a red light lit up the skull from within. Flesh reappeared on bones until a little boy stood before them. The boy lifted up his arm in appeal and blood dripped from his torn fingers. "Please don't go," he said plaintively.

Jacques Allard's face went rigid as if it had become stone. He turned away from the boy and began to walk towards the stairs.

The boy screamed and the scream became louder and nightmarish. His head flipped upwards unnaturally, revealing rows of gleaming teeth sharpened to points. He ran at Jacques and jumped upwards, sinking his teeth into the old man's neck.

The boy's arms closed around Jacques' shoulders and locked together so the man could not throw him off. Bernache ran to help, but the boy had welded to his body while his teeth continued to sink deeper into the old man's neck.

Blood squirted across the room in a jet as the boy's teeth severed an artery. Jacques' struggles became feeble as he fell to the floor. A few seconds later, he stopped moving and the boy fell from his body to become a skeleton again.

"Nothing happened here," Inspector Monde told them. "I promised the Chief Inspector that nothing would. Monsieur Allard fell down the cellar stairs and caught his neck on a piece of rubble. It is tragic that he should die in a way so reminiscent of the way his first wife did. The sooner this building is renovated the better."

The Inspector looked around at shocked faces. "Is that understood, gentlemen?"

"What about the body of the boy?" Pierre asked.

"I will see he receives a Christian burial. It will not be the first time."

Pierre and Paul walked to the stairs and numbly started to climb. Bernache stood by the Inspector looking at the two bodies on the floor.

"You were right that something powerful was coming," Bernache said softly.

The Inspector shook his head in disagreement.

"This was nothing, Louis, that thing has still to strike."

The End

Love Springs

I

Michelle Petit stared down from the side of a bridge into the swirling waters of the river Seine and wondered what she was doing there. She didn't remember coming to this place and she shivered at how cold and uninviting the river looked below. It seemed to her that she had just been falling. But that was silly because she was clearly standing on the footpath over the bridge, looking down.

Why had she come here in the first place? It must be something to do with Guy. Guy Assemard was her lover. Michelle was twenty years old while Guy was a mature twenty-eight. She was a student and he was already a qualified architect getting a reputation as both an innovator and a man to watch. He swept her off her feet from the very start, taking her to the most stylish parties and wooing her with the finest champagne.

Michelle backed away from the edge of the bridge feeling something akin to fear and began to run down the path towards Guy's apartment. For some reason she could not name she had to check that Guy was there. It could not wait another second.

Louis Bernache backed into the Inspector's office with two full mugs of coffee. He had filled them a little too full and he was scared they were going to spill as he walked. Bernache made them both with milk as he felt the Inspector was not eating enough. It was certain he had not been sleeping.

"Coffee, Inspector," Bernache said cheerfully. Inspector Monde scratched his head with one hand while holding a pen in the other. Whatever he was trying to write was not going well.

"Thank you, Louis. I could do with a break. The Chief Inspector and the Commissioner are not pleased with me over the Allard affair. Apparently their wives are furious Jacques Allard is dead and both men wish to make me feel as unhappy as they are."

Bernache nodded glumly. He sat down on the horrible plastic and tubular steel chair just in front of the Inspector's desk.

"Eve has been making my life hell too. How can a woman be so obsessed with something as trivial as a hat? Eve assures me she will never be able to go out in society again now that Monsieur Allard is dead. Apparently only his hats could show her face at its best."

"Do you regret what we did?" the Inspector asked, curious to hear his subordinate's answer. "The blame, if blame there is, is all mine, of course. I suspected the ghost was his son. I could not be certain he had killed him until I got him into the cellar. On the other hand, we had no other suspects."

"He deserved to die for what he did. I still can hardly believe a man could do that to a child, let alone his own," Bernache pursed his lips as he remembered the horror of Jacques Allard's death. "I would do it again. If France is not home to justice, what would be its purpose?"

"I thought the purpose of France in the world was to make films about people having affairs and not enjoying them," Inspector Monde said dryly. "I hope Jacques Tati will make another film soon, it has been three years since *Mon Oncle* and it is exactly that long since I laughed in a movie theatre."

"You are sometimes a very strange man, Inspector."

"Appearances are not always deceptive," Inspector Monde replied with a grin on his face. Louis Bernache laughed.

There was a knock and Sergeant Girard poked his head around the door. "Sorry to disturb you, sir, but we have a young woman at the front desk who demands to see someone of importance. If you are not too busy…?"

Inspector Monde pushed the papers he had been working on off his desk and into the wastepaper bin at its side. "As you can see Girard, I am unoccupied at the moment and would be delighted to see this young woman of yours."

Girard nodded and withdrew from the room. Bernache stood up and reached for the waste bin to recover the papers but Inspector Monde stopped him.

"They will not fire me for failing to fill out their forms, Louis. Who would they get to handle their delicate cases if they did? Let the papers remain in there; our leaders will soon get tired of asking me for them and will make something up on their own. It is better that way; they only know a small part of the truth."

"Should I go?"

"No, stay. If Sergeant Girard cannot handle this woman, you can bet good money that she will turn out to be connected to our sort of case."

There was a second knock on the door and an attractive young lady with straight black hair framing a determined face entered the room. Bernache rose out of the interview chair and move to lean against the wall. He looked into the girl's eyes and was rewarded for his efforts with a feeling like a piece of ice, trickling slowly down his spine. The inspector had anticipated correctly again. There was something strange about this woman.

"Please take a seat. This is my assistant, Gendarme Bernache and I am Inspector Monde. I understand you are here on a matter of some importance?"

The woman took one look at the plastic chair and decided to keep standing. "My name is Michelle Petit and I wish to report the disappearance of my fiancé, Guy Assemard."

"Indeed," the Inspector said, leaning back in his chair and steepling his fingers. "And when exactly did your fiancé go missing?"

"Yesterday… Afternoon I think. I can't remember," Michelle replied, sounding flustered by the question.

"Do you often have trouble remembering things from the day before?" the Inspector enquired.

"No, it is very unusual for me. Guy has gone missing and nobody is even slightly concerned. I spoke to his boss earlier today, and he said Guy had a lot of appointments to attend and that I shouldn't worry. But I am worried, especially after what happened last night."

Inspector Monde inclined his head in encouragement.

"I found myself alone on a bridge over the Seine late last night. I could not remember how I got there or what I was doing there." Michelle took out a lace handkerchief and mopped her brow, as she had begun to perspire. "I just know it had something to do with Guy, and now I can't find him anywhere."

"Does his apartment look as though he has been gone for some time?" Bernache asked.

"It looks as if he had just stepped out a moment before and I have missed him. I have been back there four times today, and I could swear that things have been moved around, but he is not there. Please help me."

The Inspector reached over the desk and handed her a couple of blank filing cards. "Write his name and address on the first card and then yours on the other. We will investigate this matter and get back to you." The Inspector paused as if something had just occurred to him. "If you could also give me the phone number of his boss, that would also be useful. I want you to go home, young lady, and rest. Do not try to visit your fiancé's apartment. Wait instead for my call."

When Michelle had left the room, the Inspector turned to his assistant. "Did you feel it, Louis?" he asked.

"I felt a chill down the back of my spine when she first came in, if that's what you mean."

"There is something supernatural involved in this matter, my friend. The important question we have to answer is what this supernatural thing might be."

"Does everybody feel these things?" Bernache asked.

"You become sensitised, the more cases you deal with, the more you will feel and see," the Inspector replied. That answer was enough to send another cold chill down Bernache's spine.

"This is Inspector Monde of the police, calling from station Rue Dante. I wish to ask you about a man who works for you called Guy Assemard."

The Inspector had rung the number for Guy's boss that Michelle provided.

"This is because of Michelle, am I right?" the cultured voice at the other end replied.

"I am pursuing the whereabouts of Guy Assemard. Do you know where I can find him?" the Inspector persisted, ignoring the question.

"He hasn't told her. I told him he should, but he never listens to me. You're wasting your time Inspector. Guy is seeing a number of people, but I can't explain. I was told in confidence. Just ignore Michelle, Guy will turn up soon, I'm sure."

Inspector Monde heard a cough and looked up in surprise. He hadn't heard anybody enter the room. A pale looking young man in a dark coat was trying to catch his attention. Inspector Monde put a hand over the mouthpiece of the phone and spoke.

"Can I help you?" he asked the man politely.

"Inspector Monde, my name's Guy Assemard. I think my girlfriend Michelle has jumped off a bridge and killed herself. I can't find her anywhere."

II

The Inspector took his hand away from the mouthpiece of the phone so he could talk.

"I will call you back if I need you. Thank you for your time," he said to the man before putting the phone down. The Inspector gestured to Guy to sit in the horrible plastic chair and reached over to press a button on his intercom. "Would you come and join me in my office, Louis?"

Bernache walked into the office a few seconds later. "What can I do for…," he stopped speaking as he noticed the man in the chair. "How did you get in here? I'm sure I would have noticed if you walked past me."

"This is Guy Assemard," the Inspector said before Guy could answer the question. "He tells me he fears that his fiancée Michelle has committed suicide jumping off a bridge."

"She isn't my fiancée, Inspector. She's just a girlfriend," Guy said quickly. "I'm sorry I walked in unannounced. The sergeant at the desk pointed me at your office before I even told him what my problem was. 'See Inspector Monde' he said to me. So here I am."

Bernache looked as though he was about to say something, but the Inspector waved him to be silent.

"I shall have words with Sergeant Girard. Why would you think that your girlfriend would want to jump off a bridge? Is she suffering from emotional problems?" the Inspector asked.

Guy looked embarrassed. "Well no, I have had the problems. I've been diagnosed with terminal cancer, Inspector. I told Michelle to meet me at the bridge because I felt suicidal. I planned to engage with her in a lover's pact. So we could go together," Guy explained. "But I fell asleep in my apartment instead, and when I woke up it was morning."

"And your girlfriend, what was her name again...?" the Inspector enquired.

"Michelle Petit."

"This Michelle, she is well aware of your medical condition, and you think she could no longer take the strain?"

Guy looked embarrassed again. "Actually, I never told her about my cancer. I didn't want to worry her at first and once it was confirmed, I couldn't tell her. But she must have found out. Why else would she jump off the bridge?"

"Why indeed?" the Inspector asked. He paused for a few seconds until the silence became oppressive. "Why do you believe she is missing? Have you checked her apartment?"

"Of course I've checked her apartment. I've been there four times today looking for her."

"And when you went into her apartment, how did you find it? Was there any sign she had been in it since last night. Was the bed made, for example?"

Guy thought about the questions before answering. "Everything was neat and tidy. The bed didn't look as though it had been slept in. That's why I'm so worried about her."

The Inspector stood up. "I am sure we can resolve this matter very soon, Monsieur Assemard. In the meantime it would be best if you go back to your apartment and wait for me." The Inspector reached out and shook Guy's hand. "Until we meet again."

"Don't you need my address and that of Michelle's?" Guy asked, puzzled at being sent away so abruptly.

"Of course, my assistant Gendarme Bernache will take your details, if you would go with him?"

Bernache led Guy Assemard out of the room and to his own desk. Inspector Monde sat back in his chair and started whistling under his breath. He looked as though his mind was miles away.

"Inspector?" Louis asked, breaking Monde out of his reverie. "What was that about?"

"A good question, my friend. Tell me, how could two people such as Michelle and Guy spend all day looking for each other and yet fail to find each other?"

"It has all the makings of a farce from the theatre," Bernache conceded. "But while those things work on the stage, they could never work in real life."

"Exactly my problem, Louis," the Inspector said animatedly. "It would be impossible. And did you note that neither of them has any memory of what happened on the bridge?"

"Guy Assemard said he was never at the bridge," Bernache pointed out.

"No, what he said was that he intended to go to the bridge and that the next thing he remembered was waking up in his bed. Perhaps he went to the bridge and forgot about it."

"For one person to forget what happened to them is unlikely enough, Inspector. Surely the idea that both these people could forget at the same time is preposterous."

"Au contraire, Louis. People who are involved in terrible accidents or trauma often forget what has happened to them. If the event is traumatic enough, an event such as falling off a bridge, for instance, or of watching a loved one fall."

"Just how many ghosts do you think we are dealing with, Inspector," Bernache asked, as an icy feeling slid down his spine.

"I wish I knew Louis, I wish I knew," the Inspector replied as he returned to contemplating his fingers.

"Have you found him?" Michelle Petit asked as she opened the door of her apartment in response to the Inspector's knock.

"Perhaps, perhaps. Can I come in?"

Michelle Petit's apartment was extremely tidy. It looked as though it had been cleaned in preparation for a new tenant.

"You keep your apartment very clean," the Inspector remarked. Michelle looked at the room as if she was seeing it for the first time.

"I have always been tidy, Inspector. It is my only vice."

"There seems to be a question about your engagement to Guy, if I might ask?"

Michelle waved her left hand at the Inspector. She was wearing a gold ring on her third finger. The ring had a cluster of small red rubies set in it with a similar sized diamond at their centre.

"Guy told me not to tell anybody about it. He proposed on New Year's Eve as the clock struck twelve. He said that if we were both still alive he would marry me this New Year's Eve."

"That doesn't sound very romantic. Why would he say something like that?"

Michelle giggled, "He says a lot of silly negative things. It is just his way, Inspector. He means nothing by it."

"He is not the sort of a man who would invite you to a bridge and then ask you to jump off it with him?" the Inspector countered.

Michelle paled and she sat down rather heavily on the chaise lounge. "Why ever would you ask such a thing, Inspector? You don't believe he's jumped into the river and drowned, do you?" Michelle asked with near panic in her voice.

"I do not believe that he would do such a thing without taking you with him," the Inspector replied thoughtfully.

Michelle breathed a sigh of relief. "Well then, Guy must be safe, because I am here."

"Perhaps," the Inspector said quietly. "I wish you to meet me at this bridge tonight, at the same time you found yourself at it yesterday."

"That was midnight, Inspector. Why do you wish to meet there so late?" Michelle asked uncertainly. The thought of going back to the bridge at night was not one she relished. If she never saw another bridge again, it would be far too soon.

"Sometimes things can only be resolved if you go back to the place they started and re-enact them. I can assure you, I will not ask this of you again. Can I rely on you to come?"

Michelle considered the Inspector's request. "If it helps to find my Guy then I will do it!" she said determinedly as she made up her mind.

The Inspector rose from his chair, took her hand and kissed the back of it lightly.

"I promise that you will know where Guy is by the end of this night, one way or the other."

III

It was a quarter past the hour of eleven in the evening when the Inspector pressed the buzzer to Guy Assemard's apartment. He rang it five times before Guy opened his door. Guy still wore the coat he had been in earlier, as if he was preparing to leave the apartment at any moment.

"Have you found my Michelle?" Guy asked as he recognised the Inspector. "I need her to be with me, I miss her so much."

"Quite," Inspector Monde replied dryly. "Perhaps, if I could enter your apartment for a few minutes and we could talk?"

Guy led the Inspector into his lounge. Guy's apartment was the opposite of Michelle's. Cushions were scattered on the floor and there were ring marks on the polished wood coffee table. It looked as if someone had hastily tidied up the room but hadn't done a particularly good job.

"So tell me Inspector, have you found Michelle?" Guy asked as they sat down.

"I know where she will be later tonight, if that is of any help."

"Wonderful. Then I can go and get her. Where will she be, Inspector?"

"You were not quite honest with me earlier. You said you were not engaged to be married to Michelle. However, I understand she is wearing the ring you gave her."

Guy flushed with sudden anger. "That is none of your business, Inspector. Michelle misunderstood what I meant when I bought her that ring. It is an eternity ring. She is mine now, to take wherever I want to take, Inspector. I never promised her marriage."

"I see," Inspector Monde said, though he didn't sound as though he told the truth.

"We will find Michelle Petit on the very bridge you were supposed to meet yesterday, at the very self-same time."

Guy got up and headed for the door.

"I will come with you," the Inspector said. "This matter cannot be considered closed until I have spoken with the young lady and assured myself she is well."

Guy turned back to the Inspector his faced once again flushed with anger. "Come if you must then, but let us hurry."

The Inspector followed Guy out of the apartment, carefully closing the door and making sure the door locked behind them.

As they walked onto the bridge a cold wind travelling along the Seine assailed them. Inspector Monde pulled his hat tighter onto his head to prevent it being blown away and turned up his collar. Guy did not seem to notice the cold as he walked determinedly towards the middle of the bridge.

A figure stood against the protective iron railing.

"Michelle?" Guy called out, running towards the shape. Inspector Monde was forced to run to catch up with him. As Guy approached the figure, he stopped. "You are not Michelle. You are the policeman who took my details."

"Good evening, Inspector," Bernache said politely. "And good evening to you, Monsieur Assemard. I see you are both out enjoying the brisk night air."

"It is a little too brisk for me tonight, if the truth be told, Louis. I am glad you were able to come," Inspector Monde said. He stood a few feet behind Guy. Bernache turned and leaned against the railings with both hands holding the top rail.

Guy turned in circles, looking desperately for Michelle. "Where is she, Inspector? What have you done with my Michelle?"

The Inspector consulted his watch, which showed there were five minutes still to go until midnight. "I am sure she will be here very soon, Monsieur Assemard. Please stop getting so agitated and wait."

"Why would she come here again?" Guy asked.

"How do you know she was here yesterday? You told us you fell asleep."

"I…," Guy stopped, unable to answer the question.

"The reason she is coming tonight is because I asked her to. I am sure you will agree, Michelle Petit is a woman who keeps her word."

A female figure could be seen against the glow of the streetlights stepping onto the bridge and walking on the other side of the road. Guy began to move forward but the Inspector stepped in front of him, blocking his path.

"You can wait until she gets here, Monsieur Assemard."

When Michelle walked close enough to see them she broke into a run. She ran past the Inspector and straight into the arms of Guy, where they embraced passionately.

"I have been so worried about you, Guy. Where have you been?" Michelle asked when they finally unclenched from their embrace.

"It is you that ran away from me, Michelle," Guy said, sounding very angry with her. "You failed me."

Michelle blanched at the tone of Guy's voice. "I don't understand. I came here last night, just as you asked."

"Perhaps I can explain things," the Inspector said quietly. Bernache moved so he stood between the two lovers and the rail of the bridge. "Guy asked you here last night to take you to your death. He planned you should both jump to your certain deaths."

Michelle gave out a bark of a laugh. "That is insane, Inspector. Why would either of us want to die?"

"I have cancer," Guy said softly and held out his hands to Michelle. She instinctively put her hands into his and gasped in shock as Guy's hands closed tight on her like a vice.

"And I need you to die with me!" he screamed as he started to pull her towards the edge.

Michelle wriggled, trying to free herself as she was dragged forward. Bernache moved behind Guy and used his body to stop him from getting to the edge. Inspector Monde put his hands around Michelle's waist and pulled her back as hard as he could.

Michelle screamed as the pain in her arms and around her waist became unbearable. She couldn't believe how strongly Guy pulled her. Bernache had been pushed back as far as he could go and used the iron railings to prevent himself being pushed into the river.

"You have to come with me!" Guy screamed. "You escaped last night and I couldn't go alone. You are mine, you bitch!"

Guy's face became more and more contorted. It looked as if it was swelling up. It was as if someone had attached a water pump and was filling him up. His eyes filled as well so his pupils looked like milk.

"Come with me!" he spluttered. Dark water poured from his mouth, soaking the surface of the bridge and making it difficult for Michelle and the Inspector to avoid slipping on it.

"You are dead, Guy!" Inspector Monde shouted. "You fell over the bridge last night after Michelle pulled herself free. You cannot take her with you, you are dead!"

Guy stopped pulling. He let go of Michelle and stared at his hands. They were swollen up and deathly white. He staggered backwards and went through Bernache, who immediately pushed himself away from the railing to stand by the Inspector.

They watched Guy as he stood against the rail, staring at his bloated hands.

"But you are mine, to do with as I please," Guy said to Michelle and again he held out his hands to her.

"I never said I would die for you, Guy," Michelle sobbed, tears running down her face.

Guy tried to lean against the railing and fell through them. The three living people ran to stare at the river below. But of Guy Assemard, there was no sign.

"Rage and anger can power a ghost to do terrible things," the Inspector said, looking at Michelle with sadness in his eyes. "But the power they have is not infinite and once used the ghost will disappear to eternal rest. That is what I asked Bernache to do for us tonight, to let the ghost of Guy Assemard expend his power against the three of us. He is gone now. Guy will not bother you again."

Michelle used a lace handkerchief to dry her eyes. "I suppose I should thank you, Inspector, for you have certainly saved my life. However, I'm afraid I cannot give my thanks at this time. I have to grieve for Guy first."

Michelle Petit turned away from the two police officers and walked back along the bridge the way she had come.

"It was not really a happy ending was it, Inspector," Bernache said.

"No Louis, the truth is these cases rarely end happily. But at least she is alive."

The two men started the long walk back across the bridge in silence.

The End

Prelude

I

Inspector Monde looked at the pile of letters on his desk and sighed. Despite his best attempts to avoid publicity, too many weird people in Paris knew far too much about him, and those people loved to send him letters. In the one in his hand, a woman wrote to tell him she suspected her cat of being a werecat because it chased a dog out of her garden. She wanted him to come and examine the cat for traces of demonic possession. And this was one of the saner letters.

He threw the letter in the wicker waste bin by the side of his desk and opened the next. He read the first couple of lines before it joined the previous. The fifth letter down contained nothing but a business card. The card was glossy and black on both sides. His hand trembled and the card dropped from his fingers onto the desk.

When he collected his thoughts sufficiently, he checked the envelope the card arrived in. His name and address were written in neat cursive script in what looked like reddish black ink. Inspector Monde doubted very much it was ink.

Bernache regularly poked his head around the Inspector's door when he got in every morning. This was to check whether the Inspector needed him and whether the inspector required his usual morning cup of coffee.

Inspector Monde sat in his chair whistling tunelessly while turning a small black card over in his hands. The whistling was a giveaway that the Inspector was troubled. Bernache stepped into the office and sat down in the horrible plastic and tubular steel interview chair. It made alarming squeaking sounds but didn't collapse under him.

Monde looked up. He threw the card at Bernache and it landed in his lap. Louis looked it over carefully. If there was any writing on it, he could not see it.

"What is this, Inspector?"

"That Louis, is a membership card for the Black Moon Club. They are not given out to ordinary mortals, nor would I ever choose to meet the conditions they require for membership."

"I've never heard of it and I've been to practically every club in Paris. Eve likes to visit new places."

"I have noticed that this Eve of yours is a very expensive hobby," Monde observed dryly.

"As with owning a sports car, there are certain compensations, Inspector," Bernache responded equally dryly.

"Do you remember the stories in the newspapers about Doriane Bélanger?"

"You mean the daughter of Maurice Bélanger, the financier? She died tragically around Christmas as I recall," Bernache said with his eyes closed as he tried to remember more of the details. "She had an undiagnosed heart condition. Her father and mother set up a foundation in her memory to prevent similar deaths."

"That is the girl. She did not die of a heart condition. I killed her."

Bernache's eyes opened wide in shock, "You killed her?"

"I asked her to drink some holy water I took from a font in Saint-Gervais."

"Holy water doesn't kill people," Bernache said and started grinning as he realised the Inspector was pulling his leg. "Unless it was a horror movie and she was a…"

"Exactly, Louis. I was asked by the Commissioner to find the girl and I tracked her down to where she was imprisoned. I thought I arrived early enough to save her life. The water was a test and she appeared to pass it at first. Sadly, it turned out I was too late."

"But such creatures do not exist."

"Did you believe in ghosts before you started working for me?" the Inspector retorted.

Bernache sat back in the groaning chair feeling stunned. The strange world the Inspector had lifted a corner of had suddenly become much darker.

"And of the card?"

"I found the girl by going to that club. Its proprietor assured me that they had rules and this case was an aberration. I decided to leave the club alone."

"But why, Inspector? Surely you should have closed it down?"

"If you find a nest of snakes doing no harm, do you go in and stir them up, spreading them out into the night, or do you leave well enough alone? I made my choice and must live it."

"Why would they send you a membership card?"

"It is an invitation, Louis. I suspect the proprietor of the club wishes me to visit him."

"I will come with you," Bernache said before the thinking part of his brain could intervene and stop him.

It was just past midnight when the Inspector knocked at the dark oak door hidden in the depths of an alleyway. Bernache stood behind him, already shivering in the cold.

A viewing slit slid open, Monde flashed the card and it slid shut. A few seconds later, the door opened and Inspector Monde and Bernache entered. They couldn't see the door attendant who stood in the shadows of the unlit hallway. The only light was dim red and came up from the stairs from the room below.

The Inspector and Bernache stepped warily down the thickly carpeted stairs.

"The doorman has just left the building," Bernache informed the Inspector when they were halfway down.

"He does that, Louis," the Inspector remarked almost cheerfully.

The room below was empty apart from the man standing behind the bar. He was very tall, thin and wearing dark clothing. In the dim red light coming from the table lamps he was almost invisible. The Inspector recognised Cervantes more by his shape than his face.

"Did you tell everyone I was coming?" Inspector Monde asked Cervantes, looking around at the empty tables.

"The club is closed and my clientele have already left Paris. I will be following them as soon as we have spoken tonight. I see you have brought a boy scout with you this time. How very appropriate."

Cervantes grinned at the Inspector and though the light was very poor; the man's canine teeth appeared longer than they should.

"This is Louis Bernache, my assistant," the Inspector said, "Louis, this is Cervantes, the owner of this club."

Bernache nodded at Cervantes. Neither man put out a hand to the other.

"You may have felt the dark growing deeper this spring, Inspector. I know you are sensitive to such things," Cervantes said conversationally. He placed three glasses on the bar and poured a viscous red liquid into each of them from a clear crystal decanter.

Cervantes noticed the grim expressions on the other two men's faces and laughed. "It is simply the finest port, I can assure you gentlemen. I bought a bottle, especially for you."

"Why did you ask me here?" Inspector Monde asked as he cautiously lifted the glass to his lips. The liquid certainly smelled like port and of a decent vintage.

"My kind has never been plentiful," Cervantes told them, as if he were discussing the weather. "A the beginning of my lifetime, we did not even know why we happened. One of us might sup from a thousand people or a thousand times from the same source and yet those people remained unchanged.

It is stupid to kill your source of sustenance, but sometimes in the ecstasy of drinking, mistakes happen. Then there would be a purge. We are vulnerable during the day and our kind would be driven out or killed. Mere belief can kill us, sacred objects, holy water, symbols of power. Believe me, we are not the threat your people make us out to be."

"My heart bleeds for you," Bernache said quietly and then blanched as Cervantes eyed him up the way a lion might an antelope.

"Then medical science came along and we discovered our kind is caused by an agent in the blood. If a human is kept short of blood and our blood given to them, they change to become one of us. Now we have the knowledge to control who joins us and who does not.

There are less than two hundred of us in the whole of Europe. There were ten of us in Paris, which is as crowded as it gets. We do not seek to increase our numbers."

"Isabella did," Inspector Monde said bleakly. He remembered the five girls in the cellar far too well. He remembered their screams as he hammered the stakes into their hearts. He knew that Cervantes was an evil creature, however reasonable he might sound.

"Most of us are happy to feed without killing or changing the humans. I am particularly fond of taking young girls as yet untouched by men. They may regret their experiences with me, but they do survive them," Cervantes ignored the Inspector's clenching fists.

"But one or two of us, like Isabella, become deranged and break the rules. They are a danger to us all and one of that kind recently arrived in Paris. That is why we are leaving, before we become caught in the crossfire."

"Why are you telling me this?" Monde asked.

"This particular one of us likes to be known as Lord Dark. It is a silly name, but do not mistake him for a fool, for he is not. He has come to Paris to humiliate and destroy you, Inspector. It would appear your reputation in dealing with the supernatural offends his sensibilities, and he was a good friend of Isabella."

"I ask you again, why are you telling me this?"

"I cannot fool you, Inspector, can I? I am telling you because he has asked me to. He has created a special message for you and given me the address where you might find it."

"I should have raided this place and burnt it to the ground, you along with it," Inspector Monde said with rare venom in his voice.

"It is too late now, Inspector," Cervantes said with a grin as he placed a piece of paper on the bar. He reached below the bar and the room was plunged into darkness. "I make sure the girls I take are at least twelve years old, Inspector. I still have some humanity."

Inspector Monde heard Cervantes leave the room. He had no trouble dealing with the lack of light.

"Has he gone, Inspector?" Bernache's hesitant voice asked.

"Yes, Louis, he has gone." The Inspector took a torch from his pocket and switched it on. He took the piece of paper off the bar and looked at it. "I think we should leave. We will need to collect the appropriate equipment before we go to visit this address."

Inspector Monde led Bernache out of the cellar. As they walked up the stairs, they heard a whooshing sound behind them as the room below burst into flames.

II

The house the piece of paper led them to was in a quiet suburb on the outskirts of Paris, well out of the Inspector's usual jurisdiction. The Inspector brought his car to a halt on the road in front of the house. Before they got out of the car the house provided a surprise for them, every one of its windows was painted black. This gave it a sinister look. Even the glass in the door was black.

The Inspector opened the boot of his car and lifted out a heavy carpetbag. The hardwood stakes inside rattled against each other setting Bernache's teeth on edge. He was still having difficulty believing in such things and in the cold spring morning light, the whole idea seemed more unbelievable than it had the night before.

Their visit to the church of Saint-Gervais earlier that morning had been surreal to Bernache. The cold feel of the hip flask against his flesh did nothing to change that. It seemed sacrilegious when the Inspector filled the two flasks from a font without asking the permission of a priest.

Bernache had concluded the Inspector must be mistaken. The man they met last night was mentally ill. He could not possibly be the real thing. Despite his new found belief, Bernache dreaded the idea of entering the house with the blacked out windows.

"I am going to talk with the neighbours before we go in. Stay here, Louis, and watch the carpetbag."

Inspector Monde chose the house on the right for no other reason than he could see its curtains were open. He knocked loudly on its front door.

A woman in her sixties answered. She had the look of a woman who missed nothing going on around her, and Inspector Monde was cheered by the prospect of talking to her.

"Yes, what do you want?" the woman asked him sharply.

"My name is Inspector Monde," Monde said flashing his identity card at her. Unlike most people, she reached out for it, dragged it closer and peered at it carefully.

"You are a long way from your police station, Inspector Charles Monde. Have I committed some crime?"

"Oh no, madam. I simply wished to enquire about your neighbours. Perhaps you could tell me why they have painted the glass on all their windows black?"

"It is a tragedy, Inspector. Their youngest child, a baby of only eight months, has developed a deadly sensitivity to natural light. Just going out in daylight could kill her. I'm told the treatment to cure her will take a number of weeks."

"Who told you this, madam? Was it the family themselves?"

"It was their physician, Doctor Dark. Three weeks ago, they painted all the windows during the night. Doctor Dark came around to the neighbours to explain. He said we must not knock at their door, as the family would have a difficult task to protect their child."

"Why could you not visit them at night?"

The woman looked puzzled for a moment, as if the question had never occurred to her. She shook her head and the puzzled look disappeared. "I'm sorry, were you saying something?"

"Can you describe this Doctor Dark?"

The woman's face went through the same expressions as before. "I'm sorry, were you saying something?" she asked again.

"Who are the family next door and how many of them are there?" the Inspector asked, wondering if this would be another question blocked in the woman's mind by Lord Dark.

"They are the family Deneuve, Inspector. A young couple with three delightful young children, Alexis who is four, Catherine who is five and not forgetting their sick baby daughter, Angelique."

"Thank you madam," the Inspector said, raising his hat politely. She closed her door slowly behind him as he walked back to Bernache, keeping her eyes on him until he left her property.

"There is a family of five in the house, Louis, or rather there was, a young couple and three children, one of them only a baby. I fear for what we may find inside."

Bernache shuddered with sudden dread. Not for the first time he wondered why he had not asked for a transfer. The Inspector moved to the door of the house with the carpetbag and Bernache rushed to catch up.

Monde tried the handle and the door opened. A small hallway became visible. Skylights above the doors would normally have let light into the house, but these were also blackened. The house reeked with the stink of the abattoir. The Inspector gagged as he stepped across the threshold and took a handkerchief out of his pocket to hold over his nose.

"Prop the front door open, Louis, and wait here."

The Inspector dropped the carpetbag in the hallway and opened it. Taking out a large hammer he stepped passed Bernache into the unpolluted air outside. He walked around the building smashing all the ground floor windows. High-pitched screams came from inside the house, but when he looked through the broken windows, he saw no one inside.

Having completed a circuit of the house the Inspector returned to where Bernache stood. Bernache appeared to have entered a state of shock.

"Get out your hip flask and remove the stopper," the Inspector commanded and Bernache reluctantly obeyed. "If anyone or anything approaches you from inside the house, throw the water over them. I shall look upstairs."

Bernache made no response except to stand across the door. The smell had dropped since the Inspector broke the windows. Monde took three sharpened stakes from the bag, putting two of them in his pocket. He took his hip flask and removed the stopper. Holding a stake in his right hand and the flask in his left, he awkwardly opened the door at the end of the hall.

As he anticipated, this door led to the stairs. He was certain there would be no one left downstairs unless they were hiding in a closet. The stairs were in near darkness; the only light coming from the hallway. The Inspector propped the door open to maximise the light and began to climb the stairs.

At the top of the stairs, he arrived at a landing with four doors leading off from it. All the doors were closed. Inspector Monde kicked the nearest door open, but the light from below was too weak to reveal anything inside. Monde knew he should go back for his torch, but instead chose to move into the darkness.

He felt an excruciating pain in his right thigh as a child grabbed him around the legs and bit him. Monde spilled some of the holy water over the child as he staggered back into the landing. A little girl with eyes as red as blood followed him out as acrid black smoke curled up from the child holding his right leg. Monde swung the flask, sending a stream of water at the girl.

She screamed in agony as the water hit her, a line of fire burned a diagonal strip across her chest. Inspector Monde fell to the floor as the weight of the child holding him dragged him down.

In the hallway below, Bernache heard the screams and the thump as the Inspector hit the floor. Then there was silence. Bernache knew he should not have let the Inspector go alone. He knew he had to do something.

Bernache rummaged in the carpetbag and found the Inspector's torch. Holding it in his left hand with the flask filled with holy water in his right he crept up the stairs. He stopped and held his breath every time the stairs creaked.

The sight on the landing was horrible enough to make Bernache want to run back down the stairs. Only the fact that the Inspector was lying on the landing stopped him.

"Are you alive, Inspector?"

"I think so," Inspector Monde replied dryly. The Inspector pushed himself up with his hands and looked around. The little girl was slumped against the side of the door. She looked like an angel, a sight only spoiled by the fact that she was cut in half diagonally. The top half of her body was three or four inches adrift of the bottom half and her organs dripped on the floor.

Inspector Monde was still being held. He twisted to look at what held him. It was a little boy, or more correctly, it was what was left of a little boy. Half the boy's head was missing. The remaining half was blackened and burned. The smell of burning flesh was nearly overwhelming.

Bernache vomited onto the stairs. He kept enough presence of mind to keep his torch pointing in the Inspector's direction. Inspector Monde pried the boy's arms from his legs. Despite the horror of the situation, he could not bring himself to kick the boy's body away.

The Inspector took the torch from Bernache's unresisting hand and swung it to look into the room where the children had been waiting to attack. What he saw there made the sights on the landing seem pleasant by comparison. Someone had gone to a lot of trouble to bind the children's mother and father with rope and hang them upside down from the ceiling.

The ceiling was sufficiently high above the floor to leave their heads dangling a metre or so above it. They had certainly been alive at that point, but they were not alive now. Their children had bitten every part of their parents they could reach to suck out their blood. They had fed so hard that the parents' heads severed from their bodies and lay on the floor. There was no trace of blood on the floor beneath the bodies; their children made sure of that.

"*Sacré bleu*, Inspector. This is evil beyond measure," Bernache spoke just behind the Inspector, causing him to drop the torch. "Sorry Inspector," Bernache said as he picked it up for him. "What could possibly be worse than this?"

As if in answer to the question, they heard the sound of a child crying. It came from one of the other rooms. The cry sounded wrong, being more like the cry of a tormented animal than that of a child.

Only one of the doors from the landing was locked. A quick search of the other rooms revealed nothing. Bernache held the torch while the Inspector kicked the door in.

The room was a nursery. Bernache's torch beam revealed wallpaper showing rabbits in clothes in jolly village scenes. The men walked over to the cot. A baby struggled beneath a single sheet, crying. The Inspector reached down into the cot to pull away the sheet.

He snatched his fingers away as a little red-eyed creature from hell tried to bite him. The Inspector checked his pockets and found he had lost his stakes.

"Louis, get me a stake from the bag."

"You cannot be serious, Inspector. It's still a baby, whatever has been done to it."

"Do you have another suggestion?"

Bernache passed the Inspector his flask of holy water. "It was quick with the children."

The Inspector saw an empty baby's bottle on a shelf beyond the cot and filled it with the water from the flask before putting the teat back on.

"Doriane told me the holy water I gave her tasted good before it killed her. Perhaps it will do the same for this poor soul."

Inspector Monde offered the bottle to the baby who took the teat in his mouth and drank greedily, little hands holding the bottle in place.

When the bottle was empty, the baby burped. Then it sighed, looked up at the Inspector and smiled. The red glow left the child's eyes and it began to cry. The crying sounded normal, but urgent.

"But how?" Bernache asked.

"I do not know, Louis. But remember what Cervantes said. It is difficult to make a vampire and it has probably never been tried with a baby before. Lord Dark must have worked hard to infect this child. Perhaps babies have more resistance than the rest of us. Perhaps they lack evil in their souls to be changed."

"Perhaps it is a miracle," Bernache said as he picked up the crying child.

"Yes, even that," Monde conceded. "We need to burn this place. I have a small can of petrol in the carpetbag that will do the job."

"Shouldn't we give this family a Christian burial?" Bernache objected.

"Would you care to explain anything you have seen here to a board of enquiry?"

The Inspector didn't wait for an answer and went to get the petrol.

Inspector Monde sat behind his desk in his usual position of contemplation. He stared at the ceiling with his fingers steepled. Bernache walked into the Inspector's office without knocking. He sat down on the plastic interview chair, ignoring its loud squeaks of protest.

"You have found a place for the baby?" Monde asked.

"At the orphanage of the Sisters of Mercy," Bernache replied in an emotionless voice.

"Not with the Nuns of the Blessed Mary?" the Inspector asked in surprise.

"They have not forgiven you for placing child ghosts with them."

"What was this all about, Inspector?" Bernache continued. "What possible message could be sent with the death of these children and their parents?"

"That is most obvious," the Inspector said, sitting back in his chair. "Lord Dark wants me to know that there are no depths of depravity he will not plumb to destroy me. No amount of effort that he is not willing to expend to achieve his objectives. It was meant to scare me."

"And does it scare you?"

"This may surprise you Louis, but it does not. I was meant to kill the baby, to taint my immortal soul with an act of barbarism. God moves in a mysterious way and instead the child was saved. We defeated Lord Dark in this, Louis. You and I defeated this creature who believes himself infallible."

"I have requested a transfer, Inspector," Bernache said dully. "The Chief Inspector has authorised a move to Lyon in six weeks' time. You will have to face this creature on your own, because I cannot cope anymore."

"It is all right, Louis," the Inspector said quietly. "I understand."

The End

Loving Hands

I

Three prostitutes stood under a Parisian street lamp trying not to let the chill get to them. It was April in Paris and it was cold, especially if you weren't wearing much in the way of clothes.

The three girls had known each other for many months. They shared the same pimp who would use his belt on them if they stepped out of line. He always hit them somewhere the marks wouldn't show. The girls tried hard to be good. It didn't stop them getting a beating though, if Nicolas thought they were slacking on the job.

Caren and Sabria were experienced and hardened. They were seventeen and Sabria first took up the life at fourteen years of age, while Caren had been on the game for almost two years. The third girl in the group was Jackie, and she'd been working as a prostitute for less than a year. She was sixteen and sometimes felt sick afterwards.

The girls were too young to work in the brothels. No brothel keeper would risk a charge of procuring sex with a child. The penalties were far too stiff. So the girls worked the dangerous dark streets instead. Thus, Paris maintained its reputation for standards in sexual matters while making life harder for the very girls they claimed to want to protect.

Jackie was thinking about her father and mother. She was a bright and sensitive girl brought up by alcoholics. Her father raped her when she was twelve. Her mother was in the bed at the time, passed out in a drunken stupor.

Nicolas was kind and considerate compared to her father, and Jackie didn't regret running away from home. Tonight was the first time she seriously wondered if she might have made a mistake.

This was the girls' first night out on the streets for two weeks. After two prostitutes had been murdered, their throats cut and bodies mutilated, Nicolas kept the girls in his apartment, saying it was too dangerous for them to be out. But two weeks is a long time if you are a pimp with a serious drug habit. He decided to send them out this night regardless of their safety. Jackie protested and nursed the bruises he gave her for talking back.

The total of murders in the area had risen to four while the girls stayed safe in the apartment. The press called the killer, Paris Pierre, and compared him to Jack the Ripper, the monster who stalked the streets of London in the nineteenth century. Paris Pierre, however, lacked the flamboyance of his English counterpart.

Some of the press moaned that the French psychopath lacked the sense of style and panache the English showed in such matters. The girls were only prostitutes after all; it was not as if important people were dying.

According to Nicolas, they should be able to make money easily. He said that, with so many prostitutes off the streets, they would have their pick of the punters and be able to charge higher prices.

It didn't work out that way. The men that usually drove slowly around the streets of Paris, seeking a need their wives or girlfriends could not satisfy, were absent. This wasn't surprising because every police officer that could be cajoled into working overtime was out trying to catch the killer.

The Police Commissioner had said the number of dead girls was unacceptable and the culprit would be caught very soon. If not, there would be new management in the homicide division.

"You'd tell the police if I went missing?" Jackie asked her friends. The thought of her body rotting in a disused alleyway disturbed her.

"Paris Pierre isn't going to kill you," Caren said and sniggered, "Unless it's because you give him bad head."

"I'm serious. I don't want my body rotting somewhere, being eaten by rats. Nobody but you would miss me if I went missing. You'd tell the police, wouldn't you?"

"Nicolas would miss your income," Sabria said as she flicked the stub of her cigarette out into the road. Its burning end traced a red arc through the air. "Young ones like you get the most clients."

"Yes, the sick ones," Caren agreed.

"Whatever," Sabria replied. "If one of us doesn't get a client soon, Nicolas is going to take it out of our hides. He can be really mean with that belt."

"I'm surprised you haven't lost it for him," Jackie said. She knew Sabria was good at getting rid of Nicolas's possessions she felt he would be better off without. In her own way, Sabria protected Nicolas from his drug habit and kept him alive.

"I lost his last belt just before you joined us, Chicken. The new one is much worse."

"Is that guy waving at us?" Caren asked, peering down the unlit street.

"Yeah, it's someone in a duffle coat," Sabria said scrunching her eyes up so she could see more clearly. "It'll bet you he wants Chicken. They always want the youngest first. Go over to him, Chicken, and see if he has money. We don't want him getting you for free, so keep your distance until you see some money."

"I'm not going until you both promise to call the police if something happens to me," Jackie said stubbornly. She thought she recognized the man as one of her clients, but she wasn't going to tell the others until she had their promise.

"Look, he's waving again. If you don't go now, you'll lose him. He's probably scared shitless of being caught by one of our heroic gendarmes," Caren said sarcastically.

"Not until you promise me," Jackie repeated.

"All right," Sabria said wearily. "We promise, if you don't come back we'll tell the police you're missing and give them a description of Robin Hood over there. Is that enough?"

"Sure," Jackie said and smiled. She ran off towards the client as fast as her high heels would carry her. She was certain she'd met him before and had lost any fear of the encounter.

"How much?" the man asked from the shadow of his hood.

The negotiation was over before it started as the man accepted Jackie's first price. She wondered if she should have asked for more. Perhaps Nicolas had been right and the lack of women on the streets had driven up the price. He was going to pay her twice as much as she usually got, and following the custom of the streets, he had already paid her half.

"Not here," he told her as she moved against him and sank to her knees. "The police are everywhere and if we get caught my wife will kill me."

"Where then?" Jackie asked wearily. If she had a franc for every time she heard a punter say something like that, she wouldn't need to be out on the streets at all.

"There's an abandoned warehouse at the end of the street," the punter told her. Jackie knew it and nodded her agreement. Provided they stayed at the edges of the ground floor, it was safe enough. The boards in the center of the rooms had rotted through and it was a long fall to the basement below.

The punter pushed a creaking door open. The owners of the building regularly boarded up the doors and windows, but they never stayed blocked for long.

As soon as she was inside the man grabbed her by the hair and started pulling her through the building. Jackie kicked and screamed as the man dragged her, but she couldn't get any purchase to break free. The punter said nothing as he pulled at her hair with increasing urgency.

When they reached the room, he kicked its door closed and forced her to her knees. Jackie felt the wisest thing to do was get on with the job and fumbled for the buttons of his fly. He struck her across her face so hard that she slid out across the rotting wooden floor.

Jackie was very frightened. If he didn't want sex then it was likely he wanted her life instead. She turned away and scrambled towards the door. The man swept her feet from under her and forced her flat on the floor. Jackie began to cry, but she wasn't crying with fear, as the bastard had succeeded in making her angry.

She remembered meeting with her father before she left home. He stood in front of her, naked from the waist down and demanded she use her mouth on him. She kicked him so hard between his legs he dropped to the floor poleaxed. She grabbed her coat and ran for her life, but not before kicking him one last time in the head, just for luck.

The man took hold of Jackie's shoulders and dragged her to her feet. She went limp to give him the idea she had given up. He relaxed his grip and she shoved him as hard as she could into the center of the room.

Her client snarled as he fell. He stood up and stamped his foot in anger. It proved to be a mistake as his foot went straight through the rotten floor and became caught in the splintered edges of the floorboards. He struggled trying to free it.

Jackie caught her breath and watched as his other leg broke through the floor when he tried to pull his first foot out. Within a few seconds, he had fallen through to his waist. Floorboards came away in his hand as he struggled to free himself.

The man stretched out his arms in appeal. "No one ever comes here. I'll die if you don't help me."

"Serves you right, Paris Pierre."

The man looked shocked. "I'm not him. I just like my sex a bit rough. I wasn't really going to hurt you. You have to believe me. Help me out, or at least tell someone I'm here."

"Go to hell!" Jackie said as she walked to the door.

"Please, please come back," the man called out as she shut the door.

Jackie leaned against the wall and shook with reaction.

II

Charles Monde sat on the hard wooden seat of the confession box and considered his life. At that moment, it seemed that it had been worth little and he had achieved nothing.

Father Francis Dubois sat in the box alongside and looked at his old friend from the little window that separated them, feeling real concern.

"The only sin you have committed since the last time we spoke is the sin of self-pity, Charles. Is this because your latest assistant has left you? Considering what you do, I find it amazing that anybody stays with you as long as a week."

Monde smiled. "No. It is true that I miss Louis, though he has not yet left the station. He has been transferred to the homicide squad until the position in Lyon becomes available." The Inspector paused for a second as he collected his thoughts.

"I will be working with him again for a little while. The Commissioner has asked that I assist in the search for this murderer, Paris Pierre, as the newspapers call him."

Father Dubois crossed himself. "Surely they do not think he is a supernatural being?"

"There had been no suspicion of such a thing until the last murder. My esteemed colleague, Inspector Morin, located a suspect he was convinced was the killer. However, the man they believed to be the killer suffered a nasty accident last week and is in hospital. Meanwhile, the murders continue."

"Is Inspector Morin the man you've described to me as a 'jackass' on a number of occasions?"

"The very same man, Francis, the very same," Inspector Monde conceded.

"So what is bothering you, Charles? Is it this Lord Dark creature?"

Inspector Monde said nothing for a long while. Father Dubois was about to repeat the question when the Inspector answered.

"Should I quit my job and leave Paris? This creature has already killed four innocents to bring himself to my attention. It is only a miracle it wasn't five. Should I run away to protect my friends from this creature's idea of fun?"

"Do you think he will strike again?" Father Dubois asked as he looked around the coffin-like confessional box. If someone wanted to kill him, the confession box would be ideal.

"I suspect he will stay away until he thinks I have dropped my guard. Then he will kill those whose deaths he believes will hurt me most."

"You plan to do nothing to stop him?"

"Of course I plan to stop him. There are people keeping their eyes and ears open looking for any sign he is in Paris. If they see or hear anything, I will know within the hour. I have arranged with the Commissioner that all police reports are scanned for signs of Lord Dark's hand. I have even set up one or two surprises if he tries to strike in the places I anticipate."

"Then why should you flee the city?"

"Because if he was to kill someone like you, I would feel it was my fault," Monde said quietly.

"It is not your fault that forces of evil exist and that God has set you on a path to fight and destroy them," Father Dubois said with conviction.

"I am not sure I believe in God."

"And you come to confession to tell me this? Charles, you are a man of many contradictions." Father Dubois leaned back on his hard wooden seat.

"Charles, I cannot set you any penance. You have done many terrible things, but always for the right reason. If you were to die tomorrow, I do not doubt that heaven would open up its doors to you without the slightest hesitation, even if you went there just to tell God he does not exist."

"I give you absolution. Go in peace, my friend and remember they have some very good priests over in Notre Dame, if you should ever feel like a change."

Father Dubois slid the little window shut and Inspector Monde got up to leave. He felt much more cheerful as he left the beautiful church of Saint-Gervais. Father Dubois was right. He wasn't responsible for the actions of Lord Dark. He just had to make sure he found Dark before he struck again.

Inspector Monde felt more than a little uncomfortable as he entered the room set up for the team dealing with the Paris Pierre murders. Black and white photographs of the bodies of the victims had been pinned to the walls and large manila folders sat beneath each set of photographs containing details of that particular victim.

A large-scale map of the center of Paris was pinned to the far wall. It had a number of red pins stuck in it, each one relating to a murder. Inspector Monde had never seen this approach before.

Inspector Morin had visited the United States of America and this was the way the FBI tackled such things. Inspector Monde thought the room was both impressive and oppressive. A man could think better with a blank wall and a cup of coffee in his hand. All the photographs on the wall did was remind a man that this particular killer was a monster.

The reason Inspector Monde felt embarrassed at entering the room was that Louis Bernache sat at one of the desks painstakingly typing up hand-written notes.

Bernache rose to his feet, pushing his chair back with a squeak. "They told me you were joining the case, Inspector. It is good to see you again," he said holding out his hand.

"I have only been down the corridor, Louis. You could have dropped by anytime," Monde pointed out as they shook hands. It would have been obvious to the densest person that Bernache had been avoiding him.

Bernache waved his arms around the room, trying to cover up his embarrassment. "This case has kept me incredibly busy. The Inspector, Inspector Morin that is, has been running us ragged. Especially after Joseph Gauthier got away from the men tracking him on the night he was injured."

"I heard something about that. They found him on the street with severe injuries to his legs, as I understand it."

"That's right. At first the Inspector thought he had been attacked by a girl, you know a prostitute, but the doctors say his injuries are more consistent with a beating or a fall," Bernache replied.

The Inspector walked over to the map. "Show me where he was found on this map, Louis."

"There's no point. It's a dead end. Another prostitute was found dead, killed in exactly the same manner two days ago, while this Gauthier man was in a hospital bed."

"Humor me, Louis. I am an Inspector of the Police, after all."

Bernache pointed out the location on the street where Joseph Gauthier had been found and the Inspector studied the map for some minutes. While he was doing so, Inspector Morin walked into the room and stood quietly behind Monde, waiting to be noticed.

"I doubt you will discover the killer by studying my back, Antoine. Though I could be wrong," Inspector Monde said dryly without turning.

"And you are not going to find him by digging up a grave at midnight," Inspector Morin replied sourly. "I have raised objections with the Chief Inspector about your presence on this case, Charles."

"Thank you for telling me that, Antoine. I am sure the Chief Inspector will pass on your request to refuse my help right up to the Commissioner, whose idea it was in the first place."

Inspector Monde turned around and faced Inspector Morin. "Did you discover where this man, Joseph Gautier received his injuries?"

"It is irrelevant, he is not the killer. When we interviewed him, he claimed some vigilantes attacked him with sticks."

"Is that a reasonable claim?" Monde asked. He had not heard of people taking the law into their own hands over this killer.

"We've had some reports of pimps punching the odd customer if they didn't like the look of him. Some of the prostitutes have taken to carrying weapons."

"That is a long way from men with sticks, Antoine."

"He is a dead end, Charles. But waste your time chasing dead ends, if you like. I shall tell the Chief Inspector you are going your own way, as usual." Morin turned away from Inspector Monde and walked out of the room in disgust.

"The Inspector is right, Inspector. It is a waste of time," Bernache said as Monde turned again to look at the map.

"I hate loose ends, Louis. They can tell you so much about what is going on when you finally clear them up." Monde sighed and turned to face his former assistant.

"Tell me about this last murder. I have heard it was different."

"Not really," Bernache replied and walked over to the latest photograph on the wall.

"This is the girl. She was seventeen years old and rather pretty as you can see from the photograph. Her real name was Catherine Perrault though that wasn't the name she used. You know these girls; they adopt false names so their parents can't trace them."

"I thought that this time, the victim was killed in plain sight?" Inspector Monde asked.

"She was killed on a street where there were witnesses, if that's what you mean. A pimp and another prostitute saw a short man in a duffle coat approach the girl and lift her into the air by her throat. By the time they got to her, the girl was dead and the man had vanished into the night."

"How could this man have done that?" Inspector Monde asked. "Did they not give chase?"

"They said he stood by the girl's body and then vanished in front of them. That's probably why the Commissioner has insisted you come on the case. But the witnesses were certainly lying,"

Bernache said wearily. "Not every crime in this city requires a ghost you know."

"So, as I said earlier, this murder was unlike the other ones."

Bernache dropped the notes he was holding onto the desk with a thump. "No Inspector, all the other girls were strangled, just like this one. We had many reports of a suspicious man in a duffle coat and hood associated with the other murders. It is the same killer."

"Not true, Louis. In the other murders, the killer made sure no one saw him commit the crime. In two of the cases, the bodies lay for days before they were found. The murderer killed in quiet secluded places until this murder. And that is ignoring the other most obvious difference."

The Inspector stopped speaking and looked at Bernache, waiting for him to point out the difference. When he did not, the Inspector waved at the other photographs.

"Look at the bruises on their throats, man. The other girls were strangled while they were kneeling and the thumb marks of the murderer turn down. The last girl was lifted in the air and the thumbs marks point upwards. You don't need to know about ghosts to spot such an obvious difference. Your team should be ashamed of yourselves."

Inspector Monde walked out of the room leaving Bernache staring at the photographs in astonishment.

III

"Go away! I am sick and tired of being interviewed by the police," the man in the bed shouted.

Inspector Monde looked him over with interest. According to the file, Joseph Gauthier was an ideal candidate to be the mass murderer.

He was a loner, going his own way and not making any friends. He was married for a short time some years before, but it didn't last. His wife left him and took their three month old child with her. Since then, he'd been arrested for assault and twice for attacking prostitutes.

Joseph worked as a joiner, making made-to-measure furniture, predominantly for a famous store in the center of Paris. He was self-employed and worked alone. According to the buyer in the store, he was dependable, but never socialized.

Physically, he was a strong man with large muscles, not too surprising given that he worked all day with his hands. At one hundred and seventy four centimeters tall, he was only a centimeter shorter than the Inspector. He was taller than the man who killed the latest victim.

Joseph lay in bed with his legs raised and bandaged. According to the nurse Monde spoke to before he entered the room; Joseph Gauthier would be released tomorrow.

"You do not like the prostitutes?" the Inspector asked, ignoring Joseph's demands.

"I can take them or leave them," Joseph replied in a disinterested manner.

"But you have punched two of them in the last year. That suggests an emotion more intense than mere indifference."

Joseph rolled over so he could look at the Inspector directly. "They assaulted me, put their hands where they shouldn't as I walked past them. I gave as good as I got."

"Many men would be flattered by their attention."

"They just wanted my money. That's all women want anyway, your money. Once they have that, you become nothing in their eyes." Joseph glowered at the Inspector.

"So why were you looking for one the night you were attacked, if I might ask? The place you were found is far away from your home or usual haunts and is known to be a place that prostitutes gather." The Inspector kept a close look on Joseph's eyes.

"I was out for a walk when I was attacked by a group of men carrying sticks. They smashed my legs and left me in the gutter to rot. I never went near any prostitutes."

The Inspector noted that Joseph blinked rapidly as he spoke, an almost certain sign he was lying.

"Did they also steal your duffle coat?"

"I don't know what you mean?" Joseph seemed taken aback by the question.

"You were seen leaving your house wearing a duffle coat with the hood raised over your head at half past ten in the evening. You were found on the street at just past midnight on the same evening without your duffle coat. What happened to your coat, Monsieur Gauthier? This is not meant as a trick question."

"I must have left it... I mean, lost it during the scuffle." Joseph looked wary, as though he had remembered where it was and didn't want to tell the Inspector.

"You said you were attacked where you were found. I can assure you that even our most ineffectual gendarme would have noticed your coat if it was there." Inspector Monde pointed out.

"You're right, Inspector. My attackers must have stolen it," Joseph said and rolled over, turning away from the Inspector. "I'm very tired. I've been severely injured, you know."

The Inspector walked out of the room and found the nurse he had spoken to earlier.

"I told you he is a nasty piece of work, didn't I," she said.

"And you were not wrong, my dear. Do you believe this man is capable of murder?"

The nurse looked at Monde and glowered. "You're all capable of it. That's what makes you a man. But that man has eyes so cold they burn when he watches me, and the way he looks makes me shiver. He would enjoy hurting a woman, I'm sure."

"You have my phone number?" the Inspector asked. The nurse fumbled in her pocket and brought out the Inspector's card, nodding her head. "I want to know when this man leaves the hospital. I gather you use specialist taxis for those who are in wheelchairs?"

"Yes, that is correct. You're going to watch this man, aren't you, Inspector? I am a little afraid, now that he knows my name and the hours I work."

"He will never attack you," the Inspector said, putting a hand lightly on the nurse's shoulder. "I guarantee it." The nurse smiled back uncertainly.

"I only saw the girl working on the street. I happened to be passing when it all went down, Inspector," Nicolas Ouellet told Inspector Monde. Since Nicolas had a record as long as the Inspector's arm for pimping, this last statement was a little disingenuous, to say the least.

They stood on the threshold to Nicolas's apartment. The man was obviously not going to invite the Inspector to come inside. Given the smell coming from the apartment, the Inspector was happy to acquiesce to Nicolas's desire.

"I do not work for the vice squad and do not care that you are a pimp, Monsieur Ouellet. But you are lying to me over a murder and I will not tolerate it," the Inspector said with menace in his voice. "If you don't tell me the truth I'll find a way to put you in prison. Do I make myself clear?"

Nicolas Ouellet looked into the Inspector's eyes and made a decision that was a first. He decided to tell the Inspector the truth.

"It was horrible Inspector. This fiend had superhuman strength and lifted poor Caren as though she was a feather. He crushed the life out of her and vanished, as God is my witness."

"Caren, Catherine Perrault was one of your girls?" the Inspector asked sharply.

"I only ever knew her as Caren, but yes she's been working for me for nearly two years," Nicolas became defensive. "I treat my girls well, Inspector. I kept them off the streets for over two weeks when the murders started, but a man has to live. I have expenses."

"After Jackie disappeared, I kept the girls in the apartment for five days, until I became desperate. This was their first night out since, and we agreed I would be on the streets with them. They would do the business where I could watch and protect them. I was doing my best to protect them."

Nicolas finished his long tirade, almost shouting. In the Inspector's eyes, he was a man strung out through a lack of drugs. The Inspector believed he kept the girls off the street until his addiction betrayed him.

"Who is this Jackie?" the Inspector asked and saw a wary look reappear in Nicolas's eyes.

"She went off with a client two weeks ago tomorrow. She didn't come back."

"You did not think to inform the authorities?" The Inspector noted that the day was the same one that Joseph Gauthier was found. "She could be lying hurt somewhere."

"Dealing with the police has not proved a pleasant experience," Nicolas replied. "My girls wanted to call the police, but I ordered them not to. They made some silly promise to Jackie not to let her disappearance go unnoticed."

"She expected to become a victim?"

"She didn't like the thought of her body rotting somewhere," Nicolas shuddered. "I understand why she said it, but once you're dead you're dead. The corpse feels nothing, only the living feel pain."

"I need to speak to your other girl. Sabria, isn't it?"

"I will take you to her, Inspector. Be gentle. She has lost her best friends in the last two weeks."

Inspector Monde followed Nicolas into his apartment. He looked at his watch. He had much to do over the next twenty four hours if he was to bring this to a satisfactory conclusion. Joseph Gauthier would be leaving hospital tomorrow evening and he had to be prepared. Most importantly of all, he had to find this girl, Jackie.

IV

Inspector Monde dragged himself into the police station at six o'clock the next morning. Louis Bernache had been in for almost an hour and watched the weary Inspector enter his office. Ten minutes later Bernache knocked on the Inspector's door carrying two cups of strong coffee.

"Come in, Louis."

"How did you know it was me?" Bernache asked as he placed the cups of coffee on the Inspector's desk and pulled up the hated interview chair to sit down. The chair groaned ominously, but Bernache had learned to ignore it.

"I saw you in the murder room. Your colleagues do not seem so eager to be working on the case."

"You're right about the murders. There are two murderers on the loose, one of whom is a copycat. The Commissioner will not be happy when he finds out," Bernache said wryly. "Inspector Morin is going to tell him later today. The rest of the team are disheartened by the news."

"The murders will end tonight, Louis. I can guarantee it. However, it is better if you know nothing more about it. You have your future career to think of."

Bernache sipped at the hot coffee and felt its thick black liquid ooze down his throat and put a warm feeling in his stomach. "You plan to do something that is not strictly legal, Inspector?"

"I intend to bring justice to those dead girls, Louis. Justice and the law only align occasionally on full moons, if at all."

"I want to help," Louis said. Inspector Monde searched the young man's eyes and saw he was sincere.

"I thought you had had enough of the supernatural?"

"We put the whole responsibility for such things onto your shoulders, Inspector. It is not right or proper. Look how tired you are."

"I spent the night searching for someone. You would never believe how many abandoned buildings there are in the center of Paris, Louis, how many places it is possible to hide the truth."

"But you have found who you were looking for?"

The Inspector nodded his head.

"Then I want to help."

It was late in the afternoon as Joseph Gauthier rolled himself out of the hospital in his wheelchair. The nurse tried to help him but he knocked her hands away.

A specially adapted taxi waited for him outside the hospital. A metal ramp allowed the wheelchair to roll into the interior of the taxi where there were straps to stop it from moving once it was inside.

A young Moroccan taxi driver stood by the vehicle and Joseph allowed the young man to push him up the ramp and show him how the straps operated.

"My name is Rico and I plan to get you exactly where you need to go," the taxi driver told him. Joseph grunted in response. He disliked foreigners almost as much as he hated women.

When the taxi began to move Joseph paid no attention to its route. The taxi was funded by the hospital and so he did not care whether it took the shortest route or not. After a few minutes of travel, he was flung violently to one side as the taxi turned into a narrow alley and speeded up.

"What are you doing, you idiot?" Joseph shouted.

"We don't want the police following us, now do we?" Rico told him from the front of the cab. He turned around to speak to Joseph, ignoring the fact he was driving and grinned. He had amazingly white teeth.

"What does it matter? They know where I live."

"But they don't know where I'm taking you. Come to think of it, neither do you." Rico turned back to watch the road. He closed the window between the front and back of the cab and locked it.

Joseph began to feel afraid. He was being kidnapped. Was the man driving the taxi a relative of one of his victims? It was possible; Joseph never discriminated against killing a girl based on the color of her skin. They all deserved to die. He clutched at the straps holding his wheelchair as the taxi rocked. If he undid the straps, he could try to get to the window. Or he could get out of the wheelchair and walk. He might manage a few steps before the pain became too great.

Rico was driving down the back streets of Paris like a lunatic and the taxi swayed from side to side. Joseph looked around for something to use as a weapon. There was a hanger for a fire extinguisher but the fire extinguisher was missing.

In the end, he sat and waited, trying to keep the wheelchair upright as the taxi swerved violently. Joseph decided to wait until the taxi stopped to try to turn the tables. Provided he was only up against Rico, he might get a chance to strangle him. Assuming Rico was foolish enough to come close. Joseph flexed his hands in anticipation.

Sabria shivered as the sun set. She was following Inspector Monde's orders. She stood at the same spot where Jackie stood with her punter the night she disappeared. His instructions were crystal clear. She was to wait until the punter who killed Caren appeared and then call out a request before the punter got close to her.

Sabria shivered again. The Inspector told Nicolas to stay in his apartment and lock his door if he wanted to live. Sabria did not doubt the Inspector knew what he was talking about. He had given them their instructions with such conviction in his voice.

The hooded figure appeared as if out of nowhere. Sabria's first attempt to speak failed as her throat was so dry, but she managed to get the words out on the second attempt.

"Take me to Jackie. I want to see her. Take me to see Jackie."

The figure in the hooded coat stood perfectly still while Sabria held her breath. Then a hand waved for her to follow and the man began walking down the street. Sabria ran to catch up, her high heels click-clacking against the cobbles as she hurried down the road.

Joseph Gauthier was not having a good day. When the taxi stopped, he found it parked beside where he had been injured. It was a building he never wanted to see again. The driver jumped out of the cab and ran off down the road.

It took Joseph a little while to figure out how to unfasten his wheelchair from the straps. A quick look through the glass showed him that Rico had taken the keys with him. After a considerable amount of fumbling, Joseph managed to open the cab door and push down the hinged ramp for the wheelchair.

As he maneuvered his wheelchair down the ramp, a familiar voice drifted across the alley.

"Well done, Joseph, you would not want to be late for the main event."

"Inspector, I've been kidnapped. You must help me to get home." Joseph demanded, but he was already sure the Inspector would do no such thing.

"I am sorry, Monsieur Gauthier. We would like you to accompany us into the warehouse, if that would not be too much trouble?" It was a rhetorical question coming from a second voice.

It took Joseph a few seconds to remember where he had heard the new voice before. "You are also a policeman. You interviewed me with the other Inspector, the stupid one."

"Louis Bernache at your service," Louis said and gave a little mock bow. Both he and the Inspector moved to stand in front of Joseph's wheelchair, blocking any possibility of escape. "I don't think police ranks are appropriate tonight."

"Louis is correct. You may call me Charles, if it helps," the Inspector said dryly.

Before Joseph could think of a reply, Bernache seized the handles of his wheelchair and pushed Joseph towards the warehouse. It was far too dark for Joseph's taste as Bernache pushed him through the building towards the room where he fell through the floor.

Joseph saw his duffle coat still lying on the floor where he left it. He shivered and looked away. As soon as he was in position, the Inspector threw a rope around Joseph's arms and chest, looping it several times around the man before tying it securely. Joseph struggled and cursed, finding he couldn't move.

"Please be quiet, Monsieur Gauthier, the main act is about to begin," the Inspector whispered. Joseph found the Inspector's words robbed him of speech. His heart pounded so fast that the sound of blood hissed in his ears. He stopped struggling and found he was listening for the slightest sound. A large rat scrabbled out from under his duffle coat on the floor and Joseph came close to screaming.

Sabria followed the hooded figure down alley after alley until they arrived at a disused building. Incongruously, there was a taxi with one of its back doors open beside it. Sabria looked around anxiously.

To her horror, the hooded figure waited at the door to the building and waved her forward again. The last place Sabria wanted to go was into a broken down warehouse with a murderer. The Inspector had been very specific with her about one thing, if she wanted to live, she must not run.

Very reluctantly, she walked forward. The hooded figure gave her a bow in acknowledgement of her bravery and disappeared into the building. Sabria followed.

They walked through the warehouse, Sabria staying several feet behind the hooded figure. Then they entered a room. The first thing Sabria saw was the dark shape of a wheelchair. There appeared to be a man sitting in it. It was all too much for her and she screamed.

The scream became a choking sound as the hooded figure turned with lightning speed and lifted her off the ground with a hand around her neck.

"Put her down, Jackie," the Inspector commanded. He moved to where he could be seen. The hooded figure hissed and dropped Sabria.

Sabria held her hand to her throat trying to massage the pain away. "Jackie? Why would you kill Caren, she was your friend?"

The hood fell back revealing Jackie's face. It was twisted with anger. She spat at Sabria's feet. "You left me to rot. After you promised me."

"They were not your killer," the Inspector said quietly.

Faster than the eye could follow Jackie covered the space to the Inspector and lifted him into the air by the throat. The Inspector tried to tell her Joseph was there, but he couldn't get the breath.

"Your murderer is in that wheelchair, Jackie," Bernache said, stepping out of the shadows. "Inspector Monde has brought him to you so that justice can be done."

The Inspector dropped to the floor as Jackie lost interest in him. She walked over to Joseph and spun the chair so he faced her. Joseph gibbered in panic.

"I came back for you," Jackie said, her voice harsh with pain. "I couldn't leave you stuck and I was worried you might fall to your death before I could get help. We managed to free your duffle coat and I used it to pull you out of the hole."

"I'm sorry," Joseph said. "I had no choice. I had to kill you."

"And I'm sorry I inconsiderately splashed my blood over your coat and you had to leave it here. I've put it to good use since."

"Bitch! I had to hamstring you first so you couldn't get away," Joseph said, anger overcoming his fear. "Spoilt the whole kill, it's nice and clean when I strangle the girls first."

"Death isn't meant to be neat and tidy," Jackie said. She moved to where the duffle coat lay on the floor and sank into it. The coat moved and then the remnants of a hand pushed the coat away covering it.

Jackie's corpse levered itself up from the floor. Most of her face had been eaten by rats and bits of flesh hung down from her jaw. Her eye sockets were black holes as the eyes were missing. Sabria screamed and fainted to the floor.

"Yes Sabria, this is why I wanted you to tell the police. Do you understand now?"

Not waiting for a response from Sabria, Jackie lurched to where Joseph sat. "What about you, Paris Pierre? Do you like the results of your handiwork? Perhaps I should perform the service you paid me for? That would be most fitting, don't you think?"

"Save me Inspector, it is your duty!" Joseph screamed as the hideous corpse knelt down beside him and started to undo the buttons of his fly.

"I'm sorry, Joseph, but you did pay for her services and it wouldn't be fair if you didn't get what you deserve."

Jackie reached for her target and pushed it into her mouth. Joseph's screams shook the building. Jackie stood up, fresh blood oozing between her teeth. "And now, how about a little kiss to end the evening properly?" she asked, leaning over to bring what remained of her mouth over his lips.

Joseph convulsed as Jackie blocked both his mouth and nose. In just over a minute his body stopped moving, as did Jackie. Her corpse lay draped over Joseph as if they were lovers snuggling together.

Bernache helped Sabria to her feet. She had missed the death of Joseph and Bernache blocked her view so she could not see what remained of him. "Go home, mademoiselle, it is over."

Sabria staggered gratefully out of the door without looking back.

Inspector Monde studied the corpses critically. "Do you think justice was done here, Louis?"

"I think justice was done, but it had nothing to do with the law."

"Let us go then, our task is done."

"What about their bodies? We can't just leave them like this."

"They will soon be found. Inspector Morin will have every man in the homicide squad out looking for the taxi outside, which is a very good reason for us to leave here now. Besides, I cannot wait to hear how the ever rational Inspector Morin is going to explain all this."

"You are a very cruel man, Inspector. I can't understand why I am going to have my transfer cancelled so I can continue to work for you."

"Neither can I, Louis, neither can I. However, it is good to have you back."

The End

Elegant Fingers

I

Inspector Morin stormed into Inspector Monde's office. Whatever he had planned to say, the sight of Louis Bernache behind the Inspector's desk brought him to a crashing halt.

"Can I help you, Inspector?" Bernache asked politely. Morin could not help but notice that Bernache was not wearing his uniform.

"Where is Monde? And why are you sitting behind his desk in civilian clothes?" Morin barked when he got over his surprise.

"The Inspector has taken a holiday on the express orders of the Chief Inspector. The Commissioner, Chief Inspector, Inspector, and I met together earlier this morning to discuss the Paris Pierre case." Louis Bernache grinned. "The Commissioner approved my transfer back to working exclusively with Inspector Monde and I have been promoted to detective, effective immediately. This is why I am no longer in uniform."

"Why was I not invited to this meeting? I am in charge of the Paris Pierre case, after all."

Bernache gave Inspector Morin his most wide-eyed innocent look. "I could not say, sir. Perhaps it's because you were busy at a crime scene?"

Morin snorted. "A staged crime scene, you mean! Unless I'm to believe a two week old corpse murdered a man tied to a wheelchair. How can Monde take a holiday with two serial killers still at large?"

Bernache put his feet up on the Inspector's table and pressed his fingers together as he had seen Inspector Monde do so many times. "I think you'll find there will be no more murders of prostitutes, at least not by Paris Pierre or his copycat."

"I forced the best pathologist in Paris to physically attend the crime scene. Do you know what the famous Dr Jean-Paul DePaul said after he had examined the bodies?" Morin blustered.

"No sir, I was not there."

"He described what the corpse supposedly did to Gauthier, which was unspeakable. Then he laughed and said 'I can see Charles's hands all over this one.'"

Bernache raised an eyebrow in what he hoped was a skeptical fashion. "Charles de Gaulle? Surely, you are not implicating the President of the Republic in these murders. Have you verified his whereabouts?"

"I believe he was referring to your boss, Inspector Charles Monde," Morin said. "And do not treat me like an idiot, Bernache, or I'll have you back in uniform before you can blink."

"Inspector Monde was with me most of last night, Inspector, and I will swear to that in court." Bernache took his feet of the desk and sat up. "I have some good advice for you, Inspector. The killer, Paris Pierre and his copycat, are gone. You have two dead bodies, one of whom was your prime suspect for all but the last of the murders. The other body could well be the one who murdered the last girl."

"Had the corpse not been a victim herself of Paris Pierre and been dead at the time!" Morin shouted.

"A creative man might construct a statement to the press saying the murderers killed each other, having been lovers. He might say the girl committed the last murder to take suspicion away from Gauthier, but when he refused to stop his killing, she killed him. The Inspector who tells this tale could take full credit for solving the case. Paris will heave a huge sigh of relief and life will return to normal."

"Pah." Inspector Morin snorted in derision. "And how would I get Dr Jean-Paul DePaul to go along with such an absurd story?"

"As you said yourself, his opinion of what happened is bizarre and would bring derision on him and on his office were he to voice it in public. You might also ask the Commissioner to have a quiet word with him. I've reason to believe he might cooperate for the sake of his reputation."

Morin looked Bernache over. "Are you sure you want to work for a man who gets involved in cases like this? Have you no self-respect?" Morin walked to the door, but he caught Bernache's words as he left.

"There will be no more dead girls on the streets tonight. Knowing that is worth a little loss of self-respect."

111

Charles Monde had not had a day off work in over two years and was feeling at a loss over what he should do with a whole week. The Commissioner had been quite insistent. Monde was surprised to look closely in a mirror and see how gaunt he had become. He could almost see his skull through the taut flesh, especially in the area around his eyes.

Inspector Monde visited a travel agency to see what might be on offer. Once it became clear that the Inspector did not approve of spending his time sitting on a beach, walking between hills or gambling in casinos, the pretty girl behind the desk suggested an itinerary for visiting palaces and places of interest. It was a three-day tour and started the next day. Inspector Monde was delighted as it would allow him to sit on a coach and brood when he was not discovering his country's history. He signed up on the spot.

The young girl ran down the corridor and up the stairs of the large elegant building. Designed to house royalty, no royal had trod its boards since the revolution. A man followed her, his nailed boots clicking loudly as he walked swiftly over the polished wooden boards. The man stalked her and meant to have his way with her when he caught her. She had to hurry.

The girl ran up another flight of stairs and then along another corridor until she reached the special place she had been seeking. Forgetting the danger to anyone using this particular place of refuge, she pressed the paneling on the wall in two places at the same time.

There was a loud click as the ancient mechanism engaged and a thick oak panel swung open. The girl squeezed through the gap into the hidden room on the other side and pushed the panel firmly shut, trapping herself inside this most secret of places.

She allowed herself to breathe quietly as she listened for the hated man following her.

Her heart was thudding like a steam engine as the sound of his boots went by. Once sufficient time passed and she calmed down, she sat on the high backed chair that, along with the table, was the only furniture in this secret lair.

Everybody knew about this room in the palace, the staff of the house knew, her family knew, everybody but the hateful man who chased her and made her hide in this place. He and all the others just like him who now stamped through the palace without the slightest respect for its history. The girl knew someone would come and let her out of the room very soon, but for some reason her heart continued to race.

II

Inspector Monde was feeling bored. This was the second day of the tour and he was convinced that if he walked around another chateau he would go insane. What he really found enjoyable was sitting in the coach watching the world go by.

The evening stop-overs in fine hostelries where he could drink the local wine and eat good food were excellent too. Monde felt as if years were dropping away from him. When he gazed in the mirror, he saw a man he almost recognized looking back. His eyes were no longer pools of black in the center of his skull. It was only the places they visited that dissatisfied him.

Today they were visiting a chateau deep in the countryside. Monde could not understand why someone would build a castle in such a remote place. Not that the chateau looked that much like a castle in its present form, though a single round tower from its early role remained. The Château de Chencinnes looked more like a very large mansion or perhaps even a hotel to Monde's cynical Parisian eyes.

Formal gardens were laid out in geometric patterns behind the house. They would look better in late summer Monde thought, when the roses were in full bloom.

Inspector Monde drifted into the house in the wake of his tour party. The guide was explaining that this estate started out as a hunting lodge. Then under royal patronage, it became a castle controlling the lands surrounding it. Prior to the revolution, it had been in the hands of a family so respected that when the revolution came, it was untouched by the peasants. Monde found that difficult to believe. His own experience with the poor in Paris was that they would set fire to a place like this just to see how high the flames would go.

The chateau had been restored and renovated in the nineteenth century by a wealthy lady called Louise Briçonnet. Her family lived in the chateau until late into the Second World War. The Nazis commandeered the chateau as a regional headquarters while France was under their control. Apparently, the family and their servants were allowed to remain in the house. When they upset the Nazis, the whole family was sent to a concentration camp where they died.

Inspector Monde tuned out his mind when the tour guide finished this part of his talk. Monde cared little about which paintings were bought when, or if the cracked vase on the wooden plinth was worth a fortune. Inspector Monde used a straightforward method for deciding the value of things. If he liked it, it was valuable; if he didn't then it wasn't. The Inspector considered himself to be a simple man and he considered the age of something a poor way to judge its value.

The tour moved a long way ahead of the Inspector. He stopped at a suit of armor and was wondering if anybody really wore anything so stupid. The eye slits in the helmet were so small it was wonder a man in it would be able to see straight ahead, let alone defend himself from attack.

When Monde finished with the armor, he turned a corner and came face to face with a painting of a young woman. Unlike the other paintings in the house, this one was fresh and vibrant. The others were covered in lacquer so thick that it was difficult to see what lay underneath. This painting was in subtle clear colors and looked as if it had been painted yesterday.

The young woman sat posed at a desk in summer. She wore light clothing consisting mainly of lace. She held a quill pen in her hand and was in the middle of writing a letter. The Inspector was struck by her long fingers, beautifully captured by the painter. As a child Monde wanted to be a painter but he could never get the hands right. This painter knew exactly what he was doing.

"That is a portrait of Lisa Madelaine Briçonnet, sir," a male voice said from behind. The Inspector turned to find that one of the people who guarded the rooms had spoken. The guard was a wizened old man. The Inspector suspected the owners of the house

114

saved money by hiring pensioners who would work because it gave them something to do.

"I'm sorry, that description means nothing to me."

"She was the youngest daughter of the family who owned this house during the war. Some say she was the reason the family were sent to their deaths," the old man continued. "I worked here then. I can tell you this, she was a lovely girl."

"How could this girl cause the death of her family? Was she a résistance fighter?"

"No, the Briçonnet's were not fighters. They were more concerned with such things as fine wines, the opera and the ballet."

"As servants, we didn't know everything that happened. But we did see and hear things, if you know what I mean. The Nazi Commandant was a nasty piece of work. He was handsome, if you are fond of dueling scars, but a sneer never left his face."

"The servants had to stay near the kitchens. Soldiers guarded the entrances to their command center to make sure we did. I think they feared we would sneak in and steal their plans. The family was free to roam the house provided they stayed out of the command center. The Nazis had set it up in the ballroom."

Inspector Monde wondered if the old man was going to get to the point or just drivel on, but as he was enjoying the painting he allowed the man to carry on talking.

"The Commandant set his sights on young Lisa Madelaine. She was twenty two at the time, just two years after that painting."

"He raped her?" Monde asked, trying to get the story to its conclusion.

"Oh no, sir. The Commandant tried to win her with charm and wit. Unfortunately for him, Lisa Madelaine did not like dueling scars and Nazis even less. She spurned his advances. He became angry at her disdain. One morning, the Commandant rounded up the whole family and sent them off to a concentration camp. Just like that."

"And you think this was because of Lisa Madelaine?"

"Well Pierre, the butler, saw the family off and he said Lisa Madelaine wasn't with them. He thought she fled the house when the Commandant's advances became too intense. He told me he heard the Commandant calling out to her that night."

Two floors above them, the girl waited for someone to let her out of the room. She tapped on the table with her fingers. She had waited a long time; surely somebody would let her out soon?

The Inspector's conversation with the old man was interrupted by shouting. One of his fellow tourists was being bundled down the corridor by two security guards.

"I tell you there's a girl being harassed up there!" the tourist shouted. "She's running from someone. Let me help her."

Inspector Monde held up his credentials and stopped the guards. "I am an Inspector de Police. Can I assist?"

The young man pulled his arms free. "Thank the Lord. Somebody sensible at last. I saw a girl being chased by a man up on the second floor. When I went to help her, these idiots grabbed me."

Inspector Monde looked at the guards. The taller one on the right decided to be the spokesman. "There are private areas of the chateau the public are not allowed to go. This man crossed a barrier and was heading into one of those areas when we caught him."

The young man had been looking around while the guard spoke. He saw the painting behind Inspector Monde and became agitated.

"That's the girl, Inspector. The girl in the painting, that's the girl I saw."

Inspector Monde smiled in delighted anticipation. He had worried that nothing interesting was going to happen this trip and was pleased his fears were unfounded. This was going to be fun.

III

The man's name was André Fortier and he was with a different tour group to that of the Inspector. He'd been walking through the rooms, staying on the public side of the roped off areas, when he caught a glimpse of a girl running down a corridor.

She had shown unmistakable signs that someone was chasing her, turning and looking distraught. She turned and fled up some stairs and Fornier had stepped across the ropes to give chase, planning to come to her rescue.

André followed the girl up to the second floor, while hotly pursued by the two security men. They tackled him as he reached the top of the stairs, bringing him to the ground. André claimed that from his position half in and out of the upper corridor; he saw the girl enter a room. Then the guards had dragged him down the stairs.

"Did you see this man you claim was chasing her?" the Inspector asked.

"No, but I swear I heard his footsteps behind me. Boots with nails in, clicking on the steps," André told him.

"The stairs are carpeted," the previously silent guard pointed out.

"And you are sure that this is the girl you saw?" the Inspector asked pointing at the portrait of Lisa Madelaine.

"Yes, I told you before. That's the girl."

"This girl died during the occupation, killed by the Nazis in a concentration camp," the Inspector told him. André Fortier looked confused. He stared at the painting and then at the Inspector.

"Perhaps she had a daughter?" he ventured.

The old man stepped forward.

"Begging your pardon, Monsieur Inspector, but I can assure you both that Lisa Madelaine Briçonnet was a virgin when she died."

"I don't think any of us can ever be sure a mature girl is in that state Monsieur…?"

"Jean François Beaudouin, at your service, Monsieur Inspector," the old man said making a small bow.

"Monsieur Beaudouin, but I take your point that if she had had a child you would most certainly have known about it. I suggest we should go and look at this room Monsieur Fortier says the girl went into."

"It is against the rules, Inspector," the first guard protested, but Inspector Monde ignored him and directed André to lead the way.

The procession made its way up to the second floor, André Fortier in the lead looking a little bit smug, the Inspector and

Monsieur Beaudouin following behind him. The two perplexed security guards trailed along at the back looking worried.

"This is where those two idiots brought me to the floor," André said as they reached the top of the stairs. Inspector Monde moved ahead of him and saw a long corridor stretch out into the distance. The left hand side of the corridor was interspersed with windows looking out onto the front of the house while the right hand side was made up of floor to ceiling oak paneling interspersed with doors.

"Which door did you see the girl go through?" the Inspector asked. André moved forwards confidently down the corridor before stopping between two doors.

"I could have sworn it was about here, but it must have been this other door," André said hesitantly, moving further down the corridor and opening the door. He stood in confusion at what he saw through the door.

The Inspector and the rest of the group moved closer and looked inside. Beyond the door was a nightmare of steel struts and wooden props holding the house together. The floorboards were missing and there was dust everywhere.

"This area of the chateau is being restored, Inspector," the first security guard explained. "That is why no one is allowed up here. It is far too dangerous."

"I don't understand?" André said. "I was so sure this was where she went."

"Perhaps you two guards could escort Monsieur Fortier back down to the public parts of the house," the Inspector suggested. "Monsieur Beaudouin and I will follow along shortly."

The two guards led a shaken and confused André Fortier back along the corridor and down the stairs. The Inspector had spoken with such natural authority that the two guards saw nothing suspicious in accepting his orders or noticed his desire to stay where he was.

"Out with it, Jean François," the Inspector demanded. "I saw the way you looked when Monsieur Fortier stopped between the doors. You looked as though someone walked over your grave."

The elderly man leaned against the far wall as if about to faint. "Please, Inspector, it is too horrible to contemplate and yet it makes a terrible sense. Why did none of us come and look? How could we fail her like that?"

Inspector Monde tapped his foot impatiently. "Would you care to explain?" he asked in as quiet and gentle tone of voice as he could manage.

"This floor has a hidden room, created to hide those persecuted a long, long time ago. To make sure those inside it did not come out before the coast was clear; the door could only be opened from the outside."

"Everybody knew about it, the family and all the servants. Lisa Madelaine would often lock herself in as a child and wait for a servant to open it for her. It was a game she played. If Lisa Madelaine was missing, she could always be found in the hidden room. It would be the first place any of us would look."

Inspector Monde placed a hand on the man's shoulder and gave a reassuring squeeze. "None of you could know she was there. Her family had been taken by the Nazis. You had no reason to look."

Jean François nodded his head in acknowledgement while continuing to hold back tears.

"Would you open the door for me, Jean François?" the Inspector asked. The old man shuffled to the panelled walls and pressed the two places. The panel swung open revealing a dust and cobwebbed interior. At the far end of the room was a tiny window with a small cross on a chain dangling from it.

There was a plain wooden table and a straight-backed wooden chair. Sitting in it were the desiccated remains of a young girl. Her skin clung tightly to her bones. The girl's clothes were perfectly preserved, her dress being a beautiful sky blue.

"Lisa Madelaine," whispered the Inspector.

The corpse tapped a finger in a deep indentation in the table. It turned its face towards the Inspector and smiled. Jean François gasped in horror.

"I knew if I waited long enough someone would come," said the rotting corpse in a husky dusty rasp as it turned and stood. "I have been waiting an age to be rescued and I do so want to thank you."

The corpse walked up to the Inspector, put its stretched skin and bone arms around his shoulders, and cried dry dusty tears over his jacket.

"I'm so glad you came, it was lonely here. If you hadn't come right at this very moment I'm sure I would have died."

The corpse pushed its face firmly against the Inspector's. Its eyes were prunes devoid of life and yet dust rolled down her desiccated skin in the facsimile of tears.

"Lisa, sweet Lisa Madelaine, you died so long ago," the Inspector told her. "You were running from Nazis during the war and that war is long over. Now it is time for you to rest. I want you to go to meet your parents where they await your return. You must be very brave."

The corpse backed away as if the Inspector had developed bad breath. Lisa looked at her fingers and hands, which were just skin and bone.

"Oh no, I thought my fingers were getting a lot thinner. Now I see they're thin because I'm dead." Lisa sank back into the chair with a moan of despair.

The sun shone through the tiny window and over the small silver cross on its delicate silver chain. As the shadow of the cross fell on her body it fell to pieces, fingers, arm and leg bones. They scattered and bounced as they hit the floor and crumbled to dust.

The End

Furry Friends

I

Inspector Monde felt refreshed and ready for anything as he walked into the police station on the Rue Dante. It was nine-thirty, the latest he had arrived for work since he joined the police force twelve years earlier. Inspector Monde had just returned from his first holiday for years and to his surprise, it turned out to be fun.

It took some fancy footwork to keep his name out of the newspapers when he uncovered the body of Lisa Madelaine Briçonnet in one of the great châteaux's of France. The story headlined all over the world, and the wizened face of Jean François Beaudouin stared out from every newspaper. Inspector Monde didn't begrudge the old man his place in the spotlight, 'better him than me' summed up the Inspector's view.

The sight that greeted him when he entered his own office was not so welcoming. His desk had been moved to make room for a second desk in the office. In the new desk sat a repentant looking Louis Bernache.

"It was not my fault, Inspector," Bernache blurted out before Monde managed two steps through the doorway. "The Chief Inspector said I must move in with you as I'm now a detective and there are no spare offices."

"Was there trouble over the Paris Pierre case?" the Inspector asked as he went behind his desk and sat down. As always, he kept his rumpled coat on.

"I believe Inspector Morin did cause some trouble despite the very good advice he received from a fellow detective," Bernache conceded.

Inspector Monde raised an eyebrow, "You tried giving Antoine Morin advice? Under the circumstances, I'm surprised the Chief Inspector has left us an office to share."

"I am sorry, sir. I really am."

"It doesn't matter, Louis. We will manage just fine, I am sure." Inspector Monde stared into space for a second and then looked at his colleague. "You do not have a flatulence problem, do you?"

"Oh no, sir," Bernache said quickly.

"Good. It we both had such a problem, then we might have to buy an electric fan," Inspector Monde said in a deadpan voice. When Bernache looked worried again, the Inspector grinned. "It is a joke, Louis. Welcome to the world of the police detective."

"Your young underworld contact, Rico, called you on the phone first thing this morning. He was surprised you were not already here. He would not tell me what he wanted to speak to you about, just that it was about 'that matter', whatever that means."

Inspector Monde sat up straight in his chair. "Did he leave any contact details?"

Louis Bernache sat up in his own chair as he saw the effect that Rico's message had on the Inspector. "He said he would meet you at the café at ten o'clock. What did he mean, Inspector, with 'that matter'?"

"Get your coat on, Louis, and come with me." The Inspector strode towards the door. As Bernache stumbled to his feet in pursuit, Inspector Monde turned towards him keeping one hand on the door. "That matter means Lord Dark," he said before heading out of the police station.

Bernache caught up with the Inspector at his car. The Inspector seemed intent on driving so Bernache went around the car to the passenger seat.

"Do you think Lord Dark has created more creatures of the night?" Bernache asked, shuddering at the thought. In their first encounter with the self-styled lord, he turned the young children of a family into monsters. Then he let the children feed on the blood of their parents, who he hung as living feeders from the ceiling. That was nearly two months ago and Bernache was still trying to get the images out of his mind.

"I would doubt it, Louis. This creature's ambition is to destroy me, my life, my friends and my career. It is a game for him, to prove my reputation is overrated. With such deranged creatures it is always difficult to predict what they will do next."

"What is our plan of action, sir?" Bernache asked hopefully. The Inspector always had a plan.

"We are going to see Rico at the Midnight Café. Once we know what he knows, we can consider making a plan."

II

The Midnight Café was a seedy little place run by an even seedier proprietor. It was well off the beaten track and was located down an alley otherwise devoid of shops. The only thing to its credit was that it never closed.

Inspector Monde stopped his car next to an old rusty taxicab parked directly in front of the café, up on the pavement. He and Bernache stepped around the cab and into the café. The little bell above the door tinkled merrily as they entered. It was the only merry thing in the café.

The owner of the café looked up and groaned in despair as he saw the Inspector and Bernache enter. Emile Fornier was a small fat man, whose one distinguishing feature apart from his piggy little eyes was his head, which was totally devoid of hair.

"The great Inspector Monde has brought a schoolboy with him today," Emile said as he glowered at Monde and Bernache. "Is that moustache stuck on? You don't look old enough to have grown it yourself."

"Ignore him, Louis. He's jealous you have a full head of hair," the Inspector advised. He put a hand out to stop Bernache from climbing over the counter and applying a traditional policing technique to the café owner. "The last time I was here he told me I would be doing him a favor if I closed him down. Leave him alone and let him continue to suffer."

The Inspector saw Rico sitting at the table furthest from the door. It was not the table the Inspector would have chosen as it had associations for him, but it would do. Rico nodded in acknowledgement.

"Two cappuccino's, if your machine is up to it," Inspector Monde said, dropping the right money on the counter and walking over to Rico. Bernache followed and the two men sat down. The three of them around such a small table was a little intimate and Bernache felt slightly embarrassed.

"I do not do waitress service," Emile said loudly from the counter, making a point of leaving the cups of coffee where they were. Bernache stood up to get the coffees and Emile backed away from the counter when he saw the look in Bernache's eye.

"Do you like my taxi, Inspector?" Rico said, grinning at the men as he indicated the wreck parked inches away from the café window.

"What on Earth are you doing with a taxi?" the Inspector asked. Rico was not noted for his legitimate work.

"When I drove a taxi for you I discovered it was fun to drive down narrow streets at speed," Rico explained. "So my mother bought me that cab and I have been in business for nearly a week now."

"That cab was stolen, and you were shaking a possible police tail," Bernache pointed out. "Driving a cab isn't normally like that."`

"I think that for Rico, it just might be, Louis," the Inspector said thoughtfully. "Do you not need a license to be a taxi driver?"

"Ah yes, if you pick up fares from the streets," Rico explained. "But if you respond to people's phone calls then you do not need a license." Rico handed the Inspector and Bernache a card. The card displayed the message, 'Rico's Private Hire Cars' and a phone number.

"The phone number goes to my mother. I have a radio in the cab and she can talk to me on that. My mother has recently become bedridden and answering the calls has given her a new sense of purpose. She has made a lot of friends."

"Is this word on the card 'cars' not a bit of an exaggeration?" Inspector Monde asked dryly. Before Rico could answer, he threw another question at him. "What have you heard, Rico, about Lord Dark?"

"You remember Sabria, Inspector?" Rico asked. The Inspector and Bernache nodded, she was the prostitute whose life they saved recently from Paris Pierre, the strangler.

"She is a friend of mine and she rang my mother last night to hire my cab. When I picked her up, she seemed to be nervous and upset. I asked her why and she told me a large hairy man approached her on the street and offered her a job that night. He gave her half the money in advance and it was a lot of money."

"What has this to do with Lord Dark?" Monde asked.

"I'm getting to that, Inspector," Rico whispered urgently, "And keep your voice down when you mention that name."

Bernache turned and saw Emile Fornier leaning over the counter towards them. When Emile saw Bernache had spotted him he moved away from the counter.

"This man, Lupine Wolfe, told Sabria that he had a very important visitor at his house and he would require her services. When she asked for what, Lupine replied 'You won't have to do much, my dear. His lordship prefers to do all the sucking.'"

"Sabria could be a target. I saved her life and Lord Dark wouldn't like that. Is she safe?" the Inspector asked.

"She's safe," Rico said. "If you would just let me tell the story. We went to the address and she couldn't stop shivering. Sabria told me she had become sensitive to dark forces since the incident with you, and she was certain she would die if she entered the house. After some discussion, I drove her to the railway station and put her on a train to Cannes where she has friends. She will come back when she feels it is safe."

"Very wise, Rico. Can you tell me this man's address?"

"I can do better than that, Inspector. I have the business card he gave Sabria." Rico felt in a couple of pockets before producing a card with a flourish.

Inspector Monde gave the card a quick glance and passed it over to Bernache. The card was black except for white writing on one side. The writing consisted of the name Lupine Wolfe with an address immediately below. The card looked very like the ones for the club, the Black Moon, which burned down two months ago.

The Inspector looked at Rico. "Thank you, my friend. Now go away and forget this ever happened. We will handle it from now on."

Rico looked disappointed at the news, but grinned at the Inspector. "I shall keep my ear to the ground, who knows what my mother and I might find out."

"Let's go back to the office, Louis. I don't want to rush in on this man without thought."

When the men walked back into their office, there was a parcel on Inspector Monde's desk. The parcel was the size and shape of a hatbox. It was wrapped in brown paper and tied with string.

"That arrived while you were out," Sergeant Girard said as he popped his head around the door. "Bit strange, as it was left on the police station steps."

"Did you not notice it was leaking?" Inspector Monde asked. A dark liquid had started to pool around its bottom surface.

"I am sorry, Inspector," the Sergeant said in embarrassment. "Do you want me to remove it?"

"Perhaps you could just open it for us Sergeant? It already has your fingerprints on it. There is a paperknife on my desk. Please be careful."

Not sure if the Inspector was playing a joke on him, Sergeant Girard cut the string binding the box and unfolded the brown paper packaging. There was a white cardboard box with a lid under the brown paper. As he lifted the lid, Bernache leaned forward to peer inside.

"Mon Dieu!" Bernache exclaimed, his face turning white.

The sergeant dropped the lid as though it had become poisonous. Staring up at them from the box was the head of Sabria, neatly severed from her body.

"I am sorry, Sabria," the Inspector said sadly as he peered into the box, "This was not your war."

"I have searched the filing system and contacted Interpol but there is no record of a Lupine Wolfe in any of them," Bernache said in frustration. His temper was not helped by Inspector Monde's laughter at his words.

"Louis, that name is the worst pseudonym I have ever encountered. I'm not surprised you can find no record of him," the Inspector said. "The question we must ask ourselves is whether the name is the mark of incredible arrogance on the part of this man, or simply a ruse to throw us off the scent."

The Inspector seemed to find his own remark funny and laughed cynically. "Poor Sabria might have found out the truth before she died. Get your gun, Louis, while I get mine from the safe."

The French police were issued guns and no gendarme would feel fully dressed without it; however, this was the first time Bernache had known the Inspector to carry one. There was a small safe fastened to the wall. Bernache had never seen it open before and didn't know the combination. The Inspector retrieved a small gun from inside before moving most of its contents out in search of something.

The contents of the safe consisted of small cardboard boxes, each with a handwritten label that Bernache was too far away to read. The Inspector found what he was looking for and opened a little box. It contained bullets and he filled his gun with them. He then carefully replaced all the contents of the safe and locked it.

"It is always important to prepare for every contingency, Louis, though I never expected to have to use this." The Inspector waved his gun around as though it explained everything.

"Should we not take a wooden stake or two with us?" Bernache asked nervously. "Just in case."

"We will pick up holy water from Saint-Gervais on our way to Monsieur Wolfe's address. You should note that we have no evidence against this man of any wrong doing, so we will have to tread carefully."

"Do we need evidence?"

"We cannot kill someone simply on suspicion, Louis. If we did that, we would be no better than those we chase."

Bernache felt a lot better when they reached the beautiful gothic church of Saint-Gervais. It was as if the sanctity of the building reached out to offer him solace. As they approached the font, Father Dubois appeared and walked over to them.

"We have come to refill our flasks from your font, Francis," Inspector Monde said with a grin on his face on seeing his old friend.

"I'm going to have to start charging you if you keep this up, Charles," Father Dubois responded. "I think my junior priests watch out for you. They certainly come running to me whenever you enter the church."

"You must take care, Francis," Inspector Monde said seriously. "That matter we talked about has happened and a young girl is already dead as the price of knowing me."

Father Dubois crossed himself. "I rarely leave the church grounds. Can such a creature tread on consecrated ground?"

"I doubt he can," Inspector Monde replied after a few seconds' thought. "But we can assume he has minions and who knows what they are capable of?"

Inspector Monde and Bernache made the journey to the address of Lupine Wolfe in silence. Bernache played with his hip flask, taking comfort in the knowledge that the water within could cut Lord Dark in two. He had seen the effect when Inspector Monde threw holy water at what had once been a little girl.

It was late in the afternoon by the time they reached Wolfe's house. The day was very warm. The sun beat down from a cloudless sky and Bernache felt too hot in his thick coat. The Inspector seemed unbothered by the weather and even buttoned up his coat.

Lupine Wolfe's address was a large pre-war detached house on a street of similar houses. As they approached its front door the men noted that all its curtains were drawn so no light could enter the house. Even the doors and the skylights above them were covered with thick black drapes.

Inspector Monde appeared to be completely unconcerned. He went up to the door and pressed the large brass button. They heard the incongruous 'ding dong' as a two-tone electric bell rang. After they had waited a minute or two, Inspector Monde rang the bell again.

"What do you want?" a husky voice called out. The voice was muffled by the door and thick curtain between them.

"Police to see Monsieur Wolfe!" the Inspector shouted.

"Very well," the voice said. It appeared to be receding. "The door is open. You are welcome to enter."

Inspector Monde tried the door and it opened easily. Out of the bright sunlight, the hallway was as dark as a cave. Bernache drew his gun as Inspector Monde stepped over the threshold.

When they were inside the Inspector motioned for Bernache to shut the door. The men waited until their eyes adjusted to the gloom.

"Are you two coming in or not?" the husky voice shouted in derision.

It wasn't completely dark in the house. The bright sunlight outside was strong enough to penetrate the curtains around their edges. But it was dark enough to be difficult to see and the Inspector and Bernache picked their way carefully down the hall, using their hands to locate pieces of furniture sticking out into it from the walls.

When they reached the lounge, they saw a figure outlined against the curtain of a large window.

"At last," the husky voice exclaimed and pulled the curtains open, flooding the room with blinding sunlight.

The Inspector flung his arm up across his eyes. The man vanished in an overwhelming glare of light. Bernache's gun fired close to the Inspector's ear and there was the sound of a body hitting the floor.

"My arm!" Bernache cried out from somewhere below the Inspector.

"Please do not fire guns in my house, detective. It is impolite," the husky voice intoned inches from the Inspector.

In a move that took their host by complete surprise, Inspector Monde wrapped his arm around Lupine and brought his gun up so that it pressed under the man's chin. The Inspector could see very little but he felt the man relax in his grip.

"There is no need to get upset, Inspector. I can see you have very good reflexes. I have not seriously hurt the young whelp. I just disarmed him before he could kill somebody by accident."

The Inspector's eyes adjusted to the light so he could see he was holding a curly black haired man that he presumed was Lupine. The man wore an unruly beard. He grinned at Monde showing his canines, which were of normal length. The Inspector pushed Lupine towards the window keeping the gun pointing at his chest.

Lupine put up his hands amiably, as though he was not in the least worried. Louis Bernache lay on the floor holding his wrist but was otherwise unarmed. His gun was on the floor just inches away from him.

"I'm sorry, Inspector. The gun just went off in my hand."

"It does not matter, Louis. How is your wrist?"

"It will be fine, Inspector," Bernache said though he grimaced as he said it. He picked up his gun gingerly and got to his feet facing their attacker.

129

"I take it you are Lupine Wolfe?" the Inspector asked. "You have a strange way of treating guests."

"Very few of them attempt to shoot me, Inspector. I apologize for the drama. I work in the carnivals and enjoy a touch of the dramatic. I am Lupine Wolfe, the famous Wolfman. I fight in the wrestling ring, perhaps you have heard of me?"

Inspector Monde lowered his weapon but did not holster it. "I think it is best if we start again. I am investigating the murder of a young girl called Sabria. I believe you invited her to your home last night."

Lupine grinned as though he found the question funny. "Was that her name? She was just a common street prostitute. She let me down despite what I paid her and never turned up."

"I understand you had an important guest visiting you?" the Inspector asked.

"Just another carnie, Inspector, no one of importance." Lupine flopped back into a large sofa and rested his arm casually along its back.

"I would still like to know his name."

"Lord Derrick is his stage name, he is a midget." Lupine wore a stupid grin on his face and Inspector Monde was certain he was both lying and teasing them.

"Do not leave Paris," Inspector Monde said. "We have not finished our investigations."

"I have no intention of leaving Paris," Lupine said, his grin having changed to a smirk as he realized the Inspector was about to leave his home empty handed. "I have been contracted for a job here, which will take me a little time."

When they were back in the car Bernache turned to face the Inspector. "Did you believe anything that bastard said?"

"I believe he is here on a job, Louis. A job we must make sure he does not complete." The Inspector started to whistle tunelessly as they drove back to the station. "You noticed he knew who I was even though we had never met?"

"Yes, Inspector. He was waiting for us to visit him, I'm sure. That business with the curtains was to taunt us and to prove he is not of Dark's kind."

"When is the next full moon?"

Bernache pulled out a small diary from his pocket. "It's a full moon tonight. Why do you ask?"

"You have an evening planned with Eve tonight, do you not?"

"Yes sir, we are going to the theatre, but I'll cancel it if you need me."

"You should go, but do not leave Eve alone tonight and be sure to lock your doors," the Inspector replied.

III

Inspector Monde watched Lupine Wolfe's house patiently from the comfort of his car. The sky was clear and the stars and moon were very bright. When a massive dog loped out of Lupine's gate, Monde started his car and began to follow from as long a distance as he dared. As he had feared, the dog noticed him after only a mile and ran into the nearest garden. The Inspector put his foot on the accelerator and sped off with a destination clearly in mind, hoping he had deduced the animal's intended target correctly.

The church of Saint-Gervais looked particularly beautiful against the starlit sky. Powerful floodlights lit the front of the church while the stain glass windows glowed from the light within. The church did not close up at night. People were free to wander in and pray or light a candle. The priests took turns to staff the church through the night, dispensing soup to the homeless that congregated about its doors.

Inspector Monde stepped quickly into the church and spotted a young priest standing by the confessional. When the priest saw who was approaching his complexion turned pale, but he did not run as his instincts told him too.

"Where is Father Dubois?" the Inspector demanded. His voice echoed in the church like a roll of thunder sent from God.

"Please do not shout in the church, Inspector," the young priest requested as he cowered back.

"Where is he?" Monde demanded loudly. "His life is at stake."

"He often takes a walk around the graveyard at night," the priest told him.

Inspector Monde ran through the church towards the graveyard, his shoes making a rhythmic clattering noise with the ancient tiles on the floor. The priest put out a hand and looked as if he was going to say something else, but it was too late, the Inspector was gone.

The graveyard was only lit by the moon and the stars. Large tombs and intricately carved monuments stood out as dark looming shapes between darker gravestones. The moonlight cast long black shadows making it difficult to make out the paths.

Monde saw Father Dubois some distance along a path, standing contemplating something that Monde could not see.

"Francis!" Monde shouted and the Father turned towards him. Father Dubois had barely finished turning when a dark shape rushed at him and bowled him over. The shape growled ferociously and attacked.

Father Dubois defended himself with his arm and screamed as the massive wolf bit straight through the sleeve of his cassock and then deep into his arm. Inspector Monde pulled out his gun and fired two shots at the creature but missing it because of the distance.

As the Inspector ran towards his friend, the wolf turned its head and laughed like a human. "You can't kill me with a simple gun, Inspector," it said huskily. "But do not worry; I have to kill a few more of your friends before I turn my attention to you."

The wolf turned its head away from the Inspector and back towards Father Dubois. "Time for you to die, priest," it growled.

Inspector Monde stopped on the path and took careful aim holding his small gun in both hands. With quiet deliberation, he put two bullets into the body of the beast. It shivered with shock and fell over onto its side.

Monde walked over slowly and carefully so as not to trip, his gun held two handed in front of him. He kicked the wolf with his shoe and the wolf rolled onto it back. It had changed to become half human and blood flowed from the two bullet wounds.

"How?" the wolf asked as its face changed to that of Lupine Wolfe.

"Your own arrogance in picking that stupid name and in telling me too much," the Inspector told him. "That and the fact

132

that I had some silver bullets made some years ago. I never thought I would ever need to use them."

Father Dubois staggered to his feet, clutching on to his bleeding right arm with his left hand. "We must call an ambulance, Charles."

"I don't think so," Monde said and put a bullet through Lupine's head. Father Dubois turned away in horror.

"We must treat that wound of yours," the Inspector said urgently as he noticed the blood flowing from Father Dubois arm.

"There is a first aid box in the sacristy," Father Dubois offered.

"No, we must wash it first in the holy water of the font. You have been bitten by a werewolf."

Inspector Monde dragged his friend into the church. The young priest started to run towards them when he saw the blood dripping from Father Dubois' arm.

The Inspector plunged the Father's arm deep into the holy water of the font. Steam poured out into the church in a billowing cloud as the water vaporized around the father's wound.

"What have you done to Father Dubois," the young priest shouted. "Did you shoot him?"

Inspector Monde ignored the man as he continued to hold Father Dubois' arm deep in the water of the font. The water scalded his hand, as it bubbled up around the priests wound. The bubbling finally stopped and Father Dubois pulled his dripping arm from the font.

"Is it over?" he asked the Inspector.

"Perhaps it is, for now," Monde replied.

The End

Crash

I

Marcel Arrass woke with a cry on his lips and for a few seconds could not work out where or who he was. It was long before dawn and he was sweating despite the room being cold. As he remembered who he was he also remembered the vision that woke him. The boy lying in the road, head at an unnatural angle. Marcel shivered, though not with cold. 'I am the killer,' he thought. At least the boy was not in the room with him now.

He felt afraid. Here in the bedroom of his own house the nightmare left him afraid. Sleep would not come. After hours of indecision he decided to get up and wash his face to clear the sweat off it. It could do no harm. There was a sense of something not quite right about the house. He put his hand to the light switch before withdrawing it. This was his home and he didn't need interior light to see. There was a full moon with clear sky and that was more than enough to navigate by.

He turned the tap and splashed water that dribbled from it over his face. Taking a towel from the rail beneath the sink he dabbed at his eyes before staring into the mirror.

There was a body in the bath!

Marcel turned and the body wasn't there. A water-stain darkened the enamel below the bath-taps, a smear of night spreading out like a cloak. It must have been an illusion. He turned back to look in the mirror and the body was there again. A frisson of sheer terror ran down his spine and he reached for the light switch.

Dirty amber illumination from the 30 watt bulb leaked across the room. The bath seemed empty until he once again turned to view it through the mirror. There the body was large as life, a male corpse. He stared at it in sick fascination. The body was rotting and unrecognisable. The head hung from the neck limply as maggots had nearly eaten through. It looked disgusting.

Marcel opened the medicine cabinet and took out the shaving mirror he rarely used. He stepped in front of the empty bath and held the mirror before him. The sight of grinning teeth with maggots squirming across them made him drop the mirror, and it fell into the bath, shattering into a thousand pieces. Each shard of mirror reflected part of the body that otherwise Marcel couldn't see.

He ran from the room slamming the door behind him and cowered in his bed, sheets pulled up to cover his face. He slowly calmed as the room remained silent but for his own ragged breathing and the door stayed closed.

Finally, he lowered the sheet from his eyes and stared straight into the face of the boy he had killed. He screamed relentlessly until the boy disappeared.

Shuddering, he waited for dawn. As light entered his room he resolved a plan of action.

'The Inspector will know what to do,' he thought. 'He was so kind all those months ago.'

II

Three months earlier

Louis Bernache entered the office backwards in an attempt to keep the cups of coffee from spilling.

"Louis, what is all the commotion outside?"

The Inspector's words were so unexpectedly close that Bernache jumped and espresso slopped into the saucers.

"Sacre bleu," the curse was barely a whisper, but it made the Inspector chuckle.

"I'm sorry, Louis. However, as I like my coffee cool it is not a problem."

Inspector Monde took the proffered cup and saucer and tipped the contents of the saucer into the cup. "See, all is well."

Bernache grinned and emulated the Inspector.

The Inspector raised an eyebrow and nodded to the door. "The noise?"

"A death. A boy was run over leaving Saint Mary's school."

"Is that a reason for shouting?"

"The driver of the car is distraught. He holds himself responsible."

The Inspector listened carefully. The shouting gave way to sobbing, which was thankfully much quieter.

"And was he responsible?"

Bernache shrugged. "Not as far as I know."

The Inspector returned to his chair and put his feet up on his desk. "Let us lend our fellow officers a hand, Louis. Inform Sergeant Girard that I will interview the driver of the car."

"It is only a traffic accident."

Inspector Monde smiled. "We don't have any cases at the moment and a child is dead. It would be churlish of us not to offer our services. Send in the gendarme who took the witness statements first. Then let us see if I can catch this driver in a lie."

Inspector Monde stood over the small man and looked down on him. The man sat with his head in his hands, barely able to speak coherently despite the fact that the accident took place well over two hours before.

"You are not guilty of a crime, Monsieur Arrass. You were travelling quite slowly and the boy stepped from behind a parked vehicle straight into your path. There was nothing you could have done to prevent his death."

Marcel shook his head violently. "I should have known. A boy is dead, Inspector. I killed him and I d-don't even kn-know his name."

The Inspector consulted his notes. "His name was Thierry Poulin. He was ten years old and saw his mother on the other side of the street as she made her way to collect him. If there is a fault it lies with the nun supervising the children for not making sure he could not get to the road. It was an accident, Monsieur."

"I would like to apo—... apologize to his family."

The Inspector shook his head. "They know it is not your fault, but it would not be wise to speak to them now. Perhaps you should go to church and light a candle for the family. Talk to your priest."

136

Marcel nodded. "Thank you, Inspector. You are a kind man." He stood up and offered his hand, which the Inspector shook firmly.

"If you are troubled, you may come and talk to me again." It was an unusual thing for the Inspector to say, and Monde questioned its wisdom as the words left his lips.

Marcel did not reply, but stumbled gratefully out of the door.

Bernache gave the Inspector a searching look. He had sat through the interview behind his desk offering no comment.

"I do not know why I said that either, Louis. Perhaps I am going soft in my old age."

"I have not noticed any other signs."

The Inspector took a sip from his coffee cup and made a face. "Cool Louis, I like it cool, but not cold."

"I'll go and make another."

Bernache stood up as Sergeant Girard entered the office with a man in tow. He vaguely remembered the man from the car accident. He looked older and much paler. They shook hands and Bernache felt a shiver run down his spine.

"I am sorry, Monsieur Arrass, the Inspector is attending a conference in Cannes and will be gone until the end of the week."

Marcel's face fell and he turned to leave.

"Perhaps I can be of assistance?"

Marcel turned back to Bernache and hesitated. "It is all foolishness. I am sure you would not be interested or believe my tale. I am being haunted."

Another shiver ran through Bernache. He had felt something strange from the moment he saw Arrass. He remembered the Inspector saying that the more you associated with the supernatural the more you came to see it around you.

"Come and tell me all about it. I have seen enough to know that things beyond our understanding do exist." Bernache waved his hand to indicate that Marcel should sit down. "Tell me all about it."

"It began as soon as I left this very office. I was upset about the death of the boy and went to church as the Inspector suggested. The priest who took my confession was most kind though I felt he should have ordered a greater penance than lighting a candle for the boy and his parents each day for a month."

"And you saw the boy's ghost in the church?"

"Oh no, not then. It was not until much later, after the day after I lit the last candle of my penance."

Marcel woke late and for a moment he felt confused. It must be the sleeping pills he'd taken the night before to drive thoughts of the dead boy from his mind. He remembered taking a bath and then going to bed. It seemed he drifted to bed as the drugs took effect.

He didn't remember dressing. He was late for work and his boss had had severe words with him the afternoon before. His performance had become unacceptable since the accident, Monsieur Gilbert had said. He was dismissed.

He was dismissed!

How could he have forgotten? Marcel stood on the busy street looking at the cars going past blaring their horns at each other. He didn't have a job to go to.

Marcel wandered the streets vaguely heading towards the place where the accident had happened. He listened to the excited shouts of children within the school walls and remembered how much fun it had been to be that young. Even during the war.

"Do not be sad, Monsieur."

Marcel looked down at the boy in school uniform. The boy looked up and smiled. It was then that Marcel saw the boy's neck was unnaturally twisted. He screamed and the boy vanished.

"You have seen the boy since this incident?" Bernache asked. A premonition of a revelation to come hovered in the back of his mind and he wondered if this was how Inspector Monde felt. It wasn't a nice feeling.

"Many times. It seems wherever I go he appears."

"Have you found another job?"

The question startled Marcel. He floundered for an answer.

"I have ... enough money to see me through."

"You are very lucky, Monsieur, to be in such a fortunate position."

"I own my home and my father left me enough to live on."

Bernache decided to get back onto the topic.

"Has this ghost threatened you?"

Marcel smashed his fist on Bernache's desk, rattling it. "He frightens me. Is that not enough? In my own home he puts out his hand, trying to draw me to my grave. In the park and on the street he calls to me. Calls my name as if we once were friends."

"Calm down, Monsieur. I think we shall have to go to your home to resolve this."

"Not a church, to seek an exorcist?"

Bernache stood. "I am hoping that will not be necessary. Will you take me there?"

As they left the station, Sergeant Girard crossed himself and gave Bernache a look of sympathy. Bernache had discovered recently that Girard once worked as the Inspector's assistant a long time ago so he was not surprised.

As they walked, Bernache asked Arrass if he had any relatives in the city. Marcel told him that he had a sister in Nice, but apart from that there was no one.

Marcel paused at his front door and searched for his keys, but could not find them.

"I will break the glass," Bernache volunteered and before Marcel could stop him smashed a panel in the door. When Bernache opened the door he stood at the threshold with the door held wide open.

"Should we not go in?" Marcel asked.

"Let us wait a few moments, there's no hurry."

After they had waited a while, Bernache put a handkerchief to his face and entered the house

III

"What are you looking at, Detective Bernache?"

Marcel had led Bernache to his bedroom and was surprised when Bernache insisted on opening the windows. It felt cold to

Marcel. Then Bernache insisted on going into the bathroom where he had retched into the small sink.

Bernache wondered how Inspector Monde did it. Then the thought occurred that what was once a human being would still be mostly human, at least for a while.

"I am looking at your body, Monsieur Arrass. It is decomposing in the bath."

Marcel laughed. "And what is this talking to you, Detective?"

"The ghost of Marcel Arrass who has not yet realized he is dead."

"That is what they sent me to tell you," Thierry Poulin said from the door. Bernache took a step back as he saw the state of the boy's neck.

Marcel looked at his hands and they faded so he could see right through them.

"I hear you had an adventure while I was away?" Inspector Monde asked cheerfully.

"Whoever told you that?"

"Sergeant Girard is most impressed. He was never able to take that final step."

Bernache grinned. "It was nothing. I was able to help someone to the truth, that is all."

Inspector Monde gave him an appraising look.

"And is that not the purpose of a policeman, in the end?"

The End

Letting Go

I

The Comte Lambert wrung his hands together as Pierre set the oil lamp up at the edge of the table. The table in question had been in the family for nearly three hundred years, but needs must when the devil drives and the Comte felt the devil pressing at his back that very minute.

"You are sure it will not spread?" he asked Pierre. Pierre had been his retainer since childhood and he had seen the Comte through all the heartache one man could endure and survive.

"It has been raining without let up for four days, my lord. The roof is sodden and we will call the fire service as soon as it has taken hold. There is always a risk, though." Pierre looked at the man he had raised from a child with some concern. "It is not too late to back out." He looked meaningfully down at the small boy clinging to the Comte's legs.

The Comte sighed. "We have no choice. Already the servants are asking questions, but what other option is there? We must go through with it."

The Comte disentangled the boy from his legs and knelt down to talk to him with their faces on a level. "You know what you must do, Sébastien?"

The boy nodded and his lower lip trembled. "Will it hurt?"

"Perhaps, it is difficult to say. Pain is all in the mind and the heart."

The Comte saw his son didn't understand. "No Sébastien, it will not hurt." He kissed his son who left him to stand beside the table.

"Do it," he ordered and Pierre knocked the oil lamp off the table.

Both men stood back, leaving the little boy standing with the lamp at his feet. For a few seconds it looked as though the lamp might go out. Oil flowed out of its reservoir and into the dense piled carpet while the flame flicked within its glass container. Then the flame jumped through the top of the lamp and the carpet caught fire with a soft whumping sound. Sébastien began to cry as the flames licked at his feet.

"We must leave you," the Comte told his son. The two men backed away as curtains caught fire and smoke billowed around them. Antoine began to scream as he was covered in flames.

"Mon Dieu!" the maid shouted as she entered the room and saw the boy. She put her hand to her mouth to suppress her scream. As she watched in horror the boy was engulfed in flames and lost to sight.

"There is nothing we can do," Pierre shouted and dragged the Comte back towards the massive oak doors. He reached out and pulled the girl back with them, slamming the doors closed on the other side. The fire alarms were sounding as Pierre took a mobile phone from his pocket and touched a speed dial button.

"Chateur Lambert is on fire. The Comte's son is missing. We need the fire service and an ambulance at once."

They heard the fire blazing on the other side of the doors, but only a trickle of smoke made it through to their side as the doors fitted so well to their frame. Then they heard the sound of approaching sirens.

"Everything will be all right, my lord," Pierre told the Comte, who sat huddled on the floor and ignored him.

II

Inspector Monde had his feet up on his desk and was engrossed in reading a newspaper which he held out in front of him. Chief Inspector Antoine Tessier walked into his office followed closely by the Commissioner de Police. Bernache jumped to stand to attention at his desk and coughed loudly.

The Inspector tilted the top edge of his paper down and took in the arrival of his guests. Unlike Bernache, he saw no need to stand or even move his feet from his desk.

142

"I take it you wish me to investigate the Comte Lambert case? May I enquire why? It seems like a simple accident from the report in the paper."

The Chief Inspector sat down in the plastic interrogation chair, which creaked alarmingly under his weight. Bernache gulped as he considered the consequences if it were to break.

"There is no need to stand on formality, Charles," he told Monde dryly. "After all, the Commissioner drops in on lowly inspectors every day."

Louis Bernache decided to offer his chair to the Commissioner and then moved back to stand against the wall. The Inspector reluctantly put down his paper and gazed blandly back at the two men.

"Louis, could you go and get some coffee for our guests?"

Bernache was only too grateful to be given the chance to escape and hurried from the room.

"I usually get a better reception, Charles," the Commissioner said and grinned. "It is good to see that not all of my employees are scared of me."

"Louis is scared enough for the two of us." The Inspector paused as he looked the men over. "However, when the Commission and my Chief Inspector choose to visit me in my office without prior notice, I think I can safely assume that it is you seeking a favour from me."

The Commissioner coughed in an embarrassed way, but did not deny the truth of the Inspector's words. He left it to the Chief Inspector to explain.

"The Comte Remy Lambert is an important man. He has suffered a great deal in recent years, first with the death of his wife in childbirth followed by a terrible fire two years ago in which it was a miracle his son survived and now a second fire has taken the life of that very son. It is the rumours surrounding the boy, Sébastien, that have brought us to your door."

The Inspector perked up as he took in this information. "And exactly what rumours are we talking about?"

"It's probably nothing," the Commissioner said quickly. "Just gossip."

The Inspector raised an eyebrow.

"The boy has hardly been seen since the earlier fire, almost as if the Comte was scared to let him out of his sight," the Chief

143

Inspector continued. "He was neither being tutored nor going to school. The Comte said he was teaching the boy himself."

The Commissioner broke in eagerly. "My wife was told that the boy has not been prospering and hasn't grown as a boy his age should. The servants say they hardly saw him despite the child being confined to the house like a prisoner."

The Inspector pursed his lips and was about to say something when Bernache arrived with the coffee. They sat for a while in silence as they drank.

It was the Inspector who restarted the conversation. "Being an over-protective father is not a crime as far as I know, though it may have led directly to this tragedy. I do not see why this case should require me."

"Inspector Morin believes the fire was deliberate and that the boy was murdered," the Chief Inspector said quietly. He saw the look of contempt form on Monde's face at the mention of Morin. "If you are uninterested we can always leave the case with him." The Chief Inspector stood up to leave.

"I see no reason why I shouldn't take a look," Inspector Monde said quickly, "provided the case is transferred in its entirety to me."

"Then it's settled," the Commissioner said. He stood and put out a hand which the Inspector shook. "Make sure that nothing gets into the newspapers."

Once the men left the office and Bernache had retrieved his chair the two men stared at each other, challenging the other to be the first to speak. As usual it was Bernache who cracked.

"What's the real reason we are being asked to investigate?"

Monde leaned back in his chair and considered the cracked paintwork on the ceiling. "People like you and me; we sense the supernatural that others pretend does not exist. Men like the Commissioner sense when something isn't quite right among the rich and powerful. He doesn't want Morin stirring up a delicate situation with a clumsy investigation. The Comte has powerful friends who could cause him trouble."

The Inspector leaned forward suddenly and stared at Louis, "We have no choice to be discrete about our work as we would face ridicule if it became public knowledge. The Commissioner is sending us to find out and hush up whatever has happened to the Comte's son."

Bernache was appalled. "He wants us to lie?"

"No more than we ever do, Louis. No more than we ever do."

III

The Inspector surveyed the fire-wrecked room with a baleful eye. The roof timbers thirty feet above him looked worryingly blackened by flame.

"You are sure this room is safe to enter?" he asked the Fire Investigator who escorted them into the building.

"The fire burned very intensely at ground level, but fortunately the rain we have been having lately had soaked into the roof. That and the open windows up there prevented the roof getting hot enough to catch fire."

"And yet the boy's body was totally consumed?" Bernache asked.

"Not totally, but more than you would expect from a fire of such a short duration."

The Inspector put a hand out and stopped the Investigator. "The fire took two hours to put out. That doesn't strike me as a short time."

"Most blazes like this last twelve hours or more. We were lucky to get it under control so quickly and with so little damage."

Bernache consulted a folder. "The autopsy report on the body confirms it was the Comte's son. They used dental records to confirm the boy's identity. Not enough of the body remained for any kind of visual identification."

"We found the body over here by the far wall," the Investigator said eagerly, leading them over to the spot.

"That is quite a distance from where the boy was last seen," Monde said. The table where the fire started was a good five metres from where his body was found.

"It's not unusual for people to run or stagger such distances when on fire."

"But wouldn't he have run towards his father and the door?" Bernache asked.

The Fire Investigator sounded a little exasperated as he replied. "He was on fire. People don't always think logically in such circumstances."

"Did you investigate the fire here two years ago?" Monde asked sharply.

"That was over in the west wing, it's still a ruin. I heard about it. The fire was caused by faulty wiring that should have been replaced years ago. The Comte's son jumped to safety out of a second storey window and landed without a scratch on him."

"I want to speak to the witnesses," Monde said abruptly, and walked away.

IV

The Comte, his aide de camp, Pierre Thibault and the maid, Denise Montigny were waiting for Monde in a small room decorated and furnished in 1920's style. The three sat at a small dining table. The Comte sat with his elbows on the table and held his head in his hands. Pierre Thibault, a much older man than the Comte, sat upright as if he had once been in the military. Denise Montigny sat with her hands in her lap and just looked worried.

Bernache entered the room a few seconds behind the Inspector and handed him the folder on the case.

"Will this take long, Inspector?" Pierre asked. "The Comte is grieving for his son and should be in his bed resting."

"Not long, I have only a few questions."

The Inspector turned to Denise. "It says in your statement that you heard someone screaming and when you entered the room you saw Sébastien in the flames at the other end of the room?"

Denise nodded and mumbled something.

"You are sure it was him?"

She nodded again. "I saw his face clearly through the flames. He looked like a little angel."

146

"How close was he standing to the table?"

"To one side of it, I think. He was taken by the flames just after I saw him." Denise started to sob and Pierre put his arm around her to comfort her.

"Is this necessary?" Pierre asked angrily. The Comte groaned, but otherwise said nothing.

"Mademoiselle Montigny, did you see Sébastien move?"

The girls sobs became louder, but she shook her head and that seemed to satisfy the Inspector. "You may go."

Bernache helped the girl to the door where a female police officer took her away.

The Inspector turned to Pierre. "Did you see the boy move?"

"He stepped back into the flames, though it was difficult to see."

"You didn't put that in your statement?"

Pierre snarled, "I did not think it relevant."

"Quite so. You may go."

Pierre stayed sitting. "I care for the Comte. He has been through a lot. I should stay with him."

"Detective Bernache, will you escort Monsieur Thibault out of the room?"

Bernache went around the table to take Pierre's arm, but the man shook him away and stood, pushing his chair back violently. "If the Comte is distressed by your questioning, I shall complain to your superiors."

Monde nodded amiably at Pierre's words and sat down facing the Comte. A few seconds later, Bernache returned and closed the door behind him.

"You loved your son?"

The Comte lifted his head revealing eyes red from crying. "More than anything in the world."

"Sometimes we must accept death and move on."

The Comte stared at Monde. "I lost my wife and she was everything to me, now I have lost my son. Have you ever lost anyone who was close to you?"

Monde stared back and a shadow seemed to cross his face. "I lost my wife, she was shot by the Nazi's. She was pregnant at the time."

"Then you know."

147

"I knew when I had to let her go," the Inspector said in a whisper, then in a voice so low that Bernache could barely hear it, he said, "She had to let me go too."

The Comte pushed away from the table as if he had been slapped. He stood and walked to the door. As he opened it, a little boy ran into the room and put his arms around him. "Papa, I had to come."

Bernache felt the hairs on the back of his neck rise as the Comte patted the boy's head and spoke comfortingly. "It is alright, Sébastien. I understand."

"The flames burned, Papa. They burned so hot."

"I'm so sorry, Sébastien."

"Why did you burn me, Papa?"

"I had no choice." The Comte returned to the table with his son in tow. "What will you do now, Inspector?" he asked in a whisper.

Bernache whispered in Monde's ear. "The boy is a ghost. I am almost certain of it."

The Inspector appeared to take no notice and smiled at the boy. "Can we go somewhere and talk, you and I?"

Sébastien looked at the Comte, who nodded his approval.

Bernache sat at the table feeling stunned as the Inspector took the little boy to the far side of the room and knelt down to talk to him. Their voices didn't carry at first, but then Sébastien became angry and shouted at Monde.

"No, he needs me, I have to stay."

The Inspector put a hand on the boy's shoulder, but the child shook it off. Monde used both hands to hold the boy so he had no choice but to look at him. He spoke urgently, but all Bernache could hear of the conversation was the emotion in Monde's voice.

Sébastien seemed to sag and Bernache thought he might have flickered in and out of existence. He nodded his head and Monde let him go. Sébastien walked towards them and Bernache felt a shiver run through him as he saw the boy's eyes. They were bleak and empty, like pools in a cave.

"I have to leave, Papa."

The Comte sighed and his body drooped in his chair. "Are you sure?"

"I have to go to Momma."

The Comte held out his hand and Sébastien took it. "Give her my love."

They held hands for a minute and then Sébastien pulled away. It seemed to Bernache that the Comte tried to hold on to his son, but there was suddenly nothing to hold on to. Sébastien turned and walked towards the door. He was gone before he reached it.

Bernache shook himself in an attempt to dispense the feeling of unreality. He stood and went over to the Comte. "I am arresting you for the murder of your son…"

A harsh laugh from the Inspector stopped Bernache in mid-sentence. "Nobody was murdered, Louis. The case is closed. Let's get out of this room and tell everybody to go home."

Bernache drove the Inspector back to the police station. Inspector Monde said nothing throughout the journey and finally it became too much for Bernache.

"Can I ask the Inspector why we did not arrest the Comte?"

"Sébastien died two years ago in the first fire. What the witnesses saw was Sébastien's ghost jumping from the window. The Comte did not find out until he and Pierre found the body. These things happen very rarely, Louis. His need for his son was so great he prevented the boy's spirit leaving."

Bernache felt even more confused. "Why did they arrange the second fire?"

"Sébastien died a little boy and grew no older as time progressed. Like all ghosts he could not manifest all the time. They could cover for that by keeping him at home, but they couldn't solve the aging problem. If he appeared to die, the Comte and his manservant thought they could keep him hidden."

"And you persuaded the boy to leave?"

Inspector Monde sighed. "It would not have worked, Louis."

"How can you be sure?"

"I tried it once, a long, long time ago."

The End

149

Vengeance

I

Gabrielle Charrier shivered as the man put his hands on her shoulders and guided her back to the bench to sit beside her children. She could see nothing through the blindfold and wasn't sure if it was night or day. She thought they had been held captive for at least three days, but she couldn't have said whether it was day or night.

"My husband will kill you for this. Let us go and he might let you live."

It was a wasted effort, she knew. She had been telling these men the same thing since this began and they always ignored her. As she rejoined her children she pulled at the bonds binding her hands behind her back and managed to touch her daughter's hands. They squeezed each other's fingertips

"I need to go to the toilet," Élise complained. She pulled her hands away from her mother's.

"Again?" The man sounded exasperated. Neither man ever said more than one word at a time to them and Gabrielle suspected they were disguising their voices, as if they were people she would know. The whole idea seemed absurd. But then, given who her husband was and what he did for a living, these men must be insane to have kidnapped them in the first place.

"You will have to untie my hands, unless you want to wipe my bottom," Élise said primly. Gabrielle felt her lips twitch almost into a smile. At twelve years old, her daughter had more poise and courage than she did. She was so proud of her.

Gabrielle sensed the man reaching for her daughter and helping her to her feet. It was strange how you can sometimes feel that people are close without seeing them. Her son shuffled along the bench to her and leaned across her breasts, trying to snuggle into his mother.

"Be brave like your sister, Nico," Gabrielle urged. Her son whimpered and she didn't blame him in the slightest. No ten-year-old should have to suffer like this.

She heard her daughter being taken away and the creak of the floorboards where the second man was moving about. She knew they both carried guns as she had felt cold steel barrels against her neck on several occasions. There were no shortages of pistols in Paris since the end of the war.

Nicolas sobbed quietly against her and she wondered if they were going to survive. Kidnappers often killed their victims once they received the ransom as that reduced the chances of them getting caught. Gabrielle was sure that Thierry would pay. Not for her or Élise, but for his beloved son. Then he would hunt down and kill these men, probably slowly and painfully. Gabrielle took comfort in her husband's career for the first time since she had found out what it was. He was the boss of an organised crime syndicate for a large portion of Paris and nobody crossed him twice.

There were shuffling sounds as her daughter returned.

"Hands," the man ordered and Gabrielle knew he was about to tie her daughter up again. Then she heard sounds of a scuffle.

"Serge, Mama it is Serge and Pascal holding us." Élise sounded incensed. "You are Papa's men and he will cut off your balls when he finds what you've done."

Gabrielle heard the sound of a fist striking flesh and then a crash as her daughter slid across the floor.

"Scum, you are dead!" Élise shouted from somewhere close. Gabrielle heard the fear and outrage in her daughter's voice.

"What do we do now?" Pascal Ruault asked. Serge Giraud and Pascal Ruault were her husband's most trusted enforcers and Gabrielle had known them for years. Once her daughter had named them it was easy to recognise their voices.

"Tie her up," Serge ordered and Gabrielle heard her daughter struggling with the men before she was thrown down on the bench next to her. Élise was sobbing and Gabrielle leant towards her, trying to offer comfort.

"Why are Papa's men doing this?" Nicolas asked.

"I don't know," Gabrielle said in a soothing voice. "Hush, Nico."

"Because they are traitors," Élise said angrily between sobs. "Papa will kill them for sure."

"What do we do?" Pascal asked in a whisper so loud that Gabrielle heard it clearly though he was at the other end of the room.

"I'll ask, he'll know." Serge sounded dangerously desperate to Gabrielle. This wasn't supposed to have happened and she feared for her children more than ever.

The sounds of footsteps echoed and a breathless third voice spoke. This was the first time Gabrielle knew there were three men involved.

"There are men with guns coming. Prevost's men, I recognised one of them. We have to get out of here. Do we take them with us?"

There was a long moment of silence before Serge spoke. Gabrielle held her breath as she knew their fate was being decided.

"You two go ahead. I'll deal with things here."

Gabrielle felt ice run down her spine. There had been no sentiment in that voice, simply resolution. There were more sounds of running feet and Gabrielle felt cold steel against her head.

"Spare my children," were her last words.

II

Thierry Charrier watched the prison gates swing open with mixed feelings. For all its faults this place had been his home for over ten years. He was a man who could command respect from fellow prisoners and prison guards alike, and his stay had not been totally unpleasant.

The guard at the gate nodded to him as he left. "Take care, Monsieur Charrier."

Thierry nodded back and stepped towards the black Renault waiting for him at the side of the road. Serge Giraud got out of the back of the car and rushed forward to greet him with a handshake, a hug and a brief touching of cheeks.

"It's been a long time, Thierry," he said as he led his boss back to the waiting car.

"Sometimes it takes a little longer than expected," Thierry said wearily. "But even France will not hold a man forever for killing his family's killer."

Serge shrugged expressively. "That is all behind you now. The chateau has been refurbished for your return. Even the gardens have been restored."

Thierry stopped and clenched his fists. "I have no time for gardens. It is Samuel Prevost we must deal with."

"Times have changed," Serge said apologetically. "Prevost controls everything in Paris, including the police."

Thierry didn't answer, but got into the back of the car and Serge followed him.

The driver turned his head to face them as Serge swung the door shut.

"It is good to see you out, boss," Pascal Ruault said cheerfully. "We'll soon show Prevost's people who really runs Paris."

"Drive the car," Serge snapped irritably.

As they drove to the chateau Thierry Charrier said nothing and Serge made no attempt to start up a conversation.

Serge led Thierry into the chateau that had been his home since the end of the war. The strong, tall walls that protected the grounds had been whitewashed and when they got inside the entrance hall of the house it smelled of disinfectant and wax. Every piece of furniture was in its place and polished as though someone had been living in the house every day of the last ten years. Thierry was amused at the trouble Serge had gone to. It must have taken a lot of effort to restore a building no one had lived in since the day he had been found guilty of murder.

"I have hired a cook, three maids and a gardener for the house. If that isn't enough I can hire more."

Thierry raised his hand an inch or so to get Serge to stop talking. "It's fine for now. You have done a good job, Serge. Did you prepare the documents I asked for?"

"On your desk, in your study, Thierry. As much information as I could get on Prevost's operations. All the things I couldn't get to you in prison."

"Then I will retire there to consider our next move. Are you staying here?"

Serge was caught off guard by the question. "I have a house and Pascal has an apartment in Paris."

"I want both of you to move into the chateau until I sort things out. Prevost may move against me for killing his brother." Thierry thought for a moment. "Are you armed?"

"Of course." Serge patted at his weapon in his shoulder holster.

Thierry nodded. "Good. Do not disturb me while I'm working."

Thierry stared at the documents and tried to decide where to start rebuilding his empire. Samuel Prevost had done a good job of consolidating the two crime organisations left behind when Vincent was killed and Thierry imprisoned for his murder. He was probably helped by the fact that he had been based in Naples and had no prior baggage. Nobody had reason to hate him as they would his brother, or Thierry.

However it had happened, it was done and would be difficult to unpick. Looking through the papers Thierry concluded that the Algerians were the weak link in Prevost's armour. They controlled much of the lower end prostitution and drugs. With a bit of luck they would be happy to trade a higher percentage for a change in loyalty.

Thierry heard the door to the study open and ignored it. The clink of bone china on silver told him it must be one of the maids bringing refreshments despite what he had told Serge. He felt in need of a drink so he would overlook his second-in-command's failure to follow orders. *A great leader needs men below him who can think independently*, he thought wryly. He couldn't remember if it was Napoleon or one of the English military who first said that.

While Thierry continued to study the documents the maid took items off the tray and placed them to either side of him, cup and saucer to his right and cakes to his left. She poured his coffee and added two sugar lumps and a dash of cream, exactly as he liked it.

154

Thierry would have sworn that Serge would never have noticed things like that; the man was proving to have the capacity to surprise him even after all these years.

Thierry expected the maid to go once the coffee was poured. He had caught glimpses of her body as she sorted out the tray but still hadn't looked at her properly. He slowly became aware that instead of leaving she stood patiently on the other side of his desk. He ignored her in the hope she would take the hint and go away, but she didn't show any signs of leaving. After a few minutes it got too much for him.

"For God's sake go!" he said, looking up for the very first time.

His heart missed a beat and then two or three. He stopped breathing and just stared, his eyes wide open in disbelief.

"Gabrielle?" It was his wife, just as she looked ten years before. She had a smile on her face as she looked at him.

"Try your coffee. It's your favourite blend."

Her voice was exactly how he remembered it. Despite the pleasant words her voice sounded somehow cold and distant. He reached for the cup and spilled coffee over his papers as he brought it to his lips. A part of his mind recognised that it was excellent even though most of his attention was focussed on the impossible vision in front of him.

"Splendid," he said, though the word came out as a croak.

"Good." Gabrielle turned and walked away. The coffee cup fell from fingers that had suddenly lost all feeling and hot brown liquid spread across the papers on the desk, turning them into a soggy mass.

The back half of Gabrielle's head was a bloody ruin. Part of her skull hung down, only held in place by her long auburn hair. Grey matter mingled with blood and dripped, though it vanished before it hit the floor.

Gabrielle turned back as she opened the door.

"I'll see you later. The kids are so looking forward to our reunion."

She closed the door behind her and Thierry finally became aware of the hot coffee that had run from the desk and onto his thighs.

"Mon Dieu," he cried, pushing his chair back from the desk and trying to hold his soaking trousers away from his legs.

155

When he sat down a few minutes later, he had a thoughtful look on his face.

"Charles Monde. I need to find Charles Monde."

III

Bernache fidgeted when he and Inspector Monde reached the door of the Commissioner de Police. He much preferred not be there.

"Perhaps I should wait outside?" he suggested nervously. "The summons was only for you."

The Inspector laughed, "But Louis, we are a team. Where I go, you go and there are no secrets between us." The Inspector knocked on the door loudly and reached for the handle. "Besides which, I like to put him off his guard by doing the unexpected."

The Commissioner raised an eyebrow when he saw Detective Bernache trailing behind Inspector Monde, but he said nothing and gestured for the men to sit down at a small coffee table where he joined them.

"I have had an unusual request for your services, Charles," he said as he poured cups of coffee for Monde and Bernache. "Do you remember Thierry Charrier?"

The Inspector froze for a second and then reached for his cup. "Who could forget the man who ran half the crime in Paris?"

Bernache looked puzzled and the Inspector continued for his benefit. "It was before your time, Louis. Charrier was a career criminal before the Nazi's invaded and he continued his profession until the 1950's when he killed his rival, Vincent Prevost, in cold blood."

The Commissioner smiled. "That is hardly fair, Charles. Prevost had just killed Charrier's wife and children."

"Their bodies were never found. I wasn't involved in the case, but the word on the streets was that Prevost was innocent. The jury seemed to agree as they sentenced Charrier to life imprisonment."

The Commissioner pursed his lips. "If the bodies had been found, he would have been found innocent by reason of *crime*

156

passionnel. And neither his wife nor his children have ever been seen in the years since. As it is, his sentence was recently commuted to the years he has served and he is now a free man."

The Inspector looked surprised. "That has been kept very quiet."

"Thierry Charrier is still a powerful man with many friends in high places."

"People who fear the information he has locked in his head and no doubt backed up by incriminating documents," the Inspector corrected.

The Commissioner nodded. "Undoubtedly, there will be some of that as well. But Charles, you are not being honest with me. Charrier has requested you by name and yet, according to our records you two have never met."

The Inspector frowned and stared down at his coffee cup.

"I thought there were to be no secrets between us," Bernache said into the silence that followed and Monde laughed.

"What is it that William Shakespeare said, *hoisted by my own petard?* Very well, I shall tell you. I worked with him during the war and I had no time for him then or now. His wife, Gabrielle, daughter Élise and son Nicolas deserved better than him. So did Paris."

Bernache was shocked, "You worked with criminals?"

The Inspector sighed. "Jacqueline and I were in the Resistance. Criminals have well established secret supply routes and access to explosives and weapons. We needed those assets to do our job, but we never trusted them."

"Jacqueline?" Bernache asked and the Inspector stared at the floor without answering.

"Jacqueline was Charles's wife," the Commissioner explained. "Someone betrayed her during the war and she was shot by the Nazi's."

"Betrayed..., or perhaps a chance discovery. We were never sure."

The Commissioner put a hand on Monde's shoulder. "It is a long time gone and best left buried in the past. Charrier has requested your assistance and it is that we should concentrate on. It is a chance to discover whether he plans to rebuild his empire by taking on Samuel Prevost. The last thing we want is a turf war on the streets of Paris. This is not Chicago, thank God."

"What did you do with Charrier that would make him want your help now?" Bernache asked.

Monde shook his head. "Nothing that I can think of. Jacqueline was his contact until her death. It was less suspicious if she visited Charrier and his family than if I had. After she died we had to work in a different way."

Something about the way Monde said that made the hairs on Bernache's neck rise and a shiver ran down his spine. He asked the question that he didn't really want answered.

"Inspector…? Charles, who do you mean when you say '*we*'?"

Monde looked up at him and Bernache saw tears in his eyes.

"Have you ever wondered about why there are ghosts? The thing that energises them is powerful emotion, emotions like love, hatred, revenge. When Jacqueline died I couldn't let her go and the war was unfinished. We continued… until the allies liberated Paris."

The Commissioner leaned towards Monde across the table.

"Did Thierry Charrier know about Jacqueline?"

The Inspector shook his head. "It was not something to be talked about. Gabrielle knew because they were special friends, and Jacqueline said goodbye to her before she left. Gabrielle might have told Thierry, but he would never have believed her. He is a pragmatic man and would have no time for ghost stories."

"Unless he had a reason," Bernache said quietly.

"Will you take this assignment, Inspector?" the Commissioner asked.

Inspector Monde nodded. "Not for Thierry Charrier. I would not spit on him if he were on fire. But for the sake of Gabrielle and her children's immortal souls I will investigate and see what I can do."

"And you, Detective Bernache? Will you work with Inspector Monde on this case and try to keep the reputation of the police untarnished?"

Bernache was surprised to be asked. It was his duty and this was still a police case regardless of the morality of the man asking for their help. "Yes, sir!"

The Inspector stood and Bernache followed. As they reached the door the Commissioner called out to them.

"Please remember, my secretary is a highly strung woman. There is no need to report everything that happens. All that is required is a satisfactory outcome."

"I always aim to please," the Inspector said in reply, and the two men left the room.

"Given his usual aim, Lord help us all," the Commissioner said fervently to an empty room.

IV

The Inspector directed Bernache to park their car in front of an impressive townhouse in one of the richest districts in Paris.

"This is the home of Thierry Charrier? It is impressive."

Monde shook his head. "Charrier lives to the north on the outskirts of the city. This is the home of Samuel Prevost and was the home of his brother before him, the late unlamented Vincent Prevost."

Bernache looked puzzled. "Why come here? Do you think Prevost is behind Charrier's request?"

The Inspector was about to answer when the door of the house opened and a man stepped out. The man wore a hat that served to conceal most of his face. Monde watched him walk briskly down the road and out of sight.

"Interesting. Louis, if I didn't know better I would have said that man was Serge Giraud. It's been nearly twenty years since I last saw him, but I would still swear it was him, there is something about his walk that is very distinctive. He was Charrier's right hand man and enforcer during the war."

"Does he still work for Charrier?"

The Inspector shrugged noncommittally. "Come, let us see if Samuel Prevost will speak to us. By careful what you say in there, Louis. Prevost is a dangerous man."

The two heavy set men at the door made them wait for ten minutes before they were led down opulent corridors to a study that looked as if it had been designed in the time of Napoleon

Bonaparte and left unchanged since, except for the addition of an elegant old fashioned phone that sat on the desk.

Behind the desk sat a big, well-muscled middle aged man. He wore a suit of immaculate cut with silk shirt and flamboyant cravat. He stood as they entered and offered his hand out to the Inspector.

"I have often wondered when I would get to meet the famous Inspector Monde," he said as Monde shook his hand. "You did us all a favour when you got rid of the Black Moon Club and those that inhabited it. I've been looking for the opportunity to thank you."

Monde shrugged. "Some creatures prey on us all, even criminals."

Prevost smiled. "I am a business man, Inspector Monde, not a criminal. You must have been misinformed. The great and the good coming knocking at my door all the time, as you must well know."

The Inspector ignored Prevost's words and spoke sharply. "Thierry Charrier has been released from prison. He killed your brother."

Prevost spread his hands and his smile grew broader. "He has served one sentence and will serve another for the remainder of his life. I have no interest in him."

"Even if he restarts his... *business* activities?" Bernache asked.

"I like you, Detective Bernache," Prevost said dryly, "A man who speaks his mind without thought of the consequences. Business thrives on competition, but I have little to fear from someone who is clearly yesterday's man."

"He killed your brother," Monde pressed.

"Someone would have, sooner or later. My brother made many enemies."

Monde and Bernache stared at Prevost in disbelief and he, in return, smiled blandly back. The silence stretched between them.

"If that is all you wished to ask me, I shall bid you good day," Prevost said finally. "I am a busy man, Inspector. I'm the chairman of the committee raising funds for the orphans of the city and we have a meeting scheduled in half an hour's time."

"Thierry Charrier has asked for my assistance. Do you know why?"

160

Prevost laughed. "That is most amusing. I would suggest you ask him rather than me. Perhaps he has received a black calling card."

The Inspector shrugged. "Perhaps. Thank you for your time, Monsieur Prevost. You have been most helpful."

The Inspector turned to go and Prevost coughed discreetly to regain his attention.

"Vincent did not kill Gabrielle Charrier or her children. In fact, he sent them back to Thierry Charrier in the same condition he found them. You might even say, in better condition." Prevost seemed to find his words exceedingly funny and began to chuckle.

"It occurs to me that I do know why Charrier wants your assistance, Inspector. But I think it would be best if you find out for yourself."

Bernache and Inspector Monde walked down the corridor with Samuel Prevost's laughter echoing behind them.

V

Thierry Charrier's house was in an exclusive suburb to the north of Paris. It and its gardens were surrounded by an impressive fifteen foot wall, plastered with a stucco finish and recently whitewashed. The only point of entry was a large pair of wrought iron gates that led to the drive. When the Inspector and Bernache arrived they found them padlocked closed. There was an incongruous modern plastic electric bell push below a brass plate that read. *Push the button and wait.*

Bernache followed the instructions and peered through the gates and down the road towards the house.

"It seems crime does pay after all, Inspector."

Monde joined Bernache and looked into the grounds. "Someone has been tidying up. The gardens are overgrown, but the bushes by the drive have been recently trimmed and someone has cut the grass."

"Someone is coming."

A tough looking man approached them from the direction of the house. Bernache noted the bulge beneath the man's jacket indicating he was carrying a gun. Despite wearing expensive clothes the man looked dishevelled and hadn't shaved that morning.

"Yes?"

"Inspector Monde and Detective Bernache to see Thierry Charrier," the Inspector said curtly. "We are expected."

The man grunted and reached into his pocket for the keys to the gate. "I'm Pascal Ruault, in charge of Monsieur Charrier's security. He told me to expect you. Get back in your car and drive up to the front of the house. I'll meet you there."

A few minutes later Ruault led them inside the house. A couple of large suitcases had been pushed against the wall just inside the door.

"I didn't think prisoners were allowed to have so many possessions," Bernache said as he looked at the cases.

Ruault scowled. "Those are mine and Serge's. We moved in today."

"Is Serge Giraud still working for Thierry?" the Inspector asked. "I knew them both during the war."

"I work for Serge. He and I looked after things for Monsieur Charrier while he was away."

"But not in this house?" Bernache enquired.

"This is Monsieur Charrier's home. It was looked after by a caretaker while he was away. But even the caretaker didn't live here. Serge hired live-in servants when we learnt Monsieur Charrier was about to be released."

Bernache was about to ask another question when the Inspector gave a small shake of his head.

Ruault led them deeper into the house. It was an eerily quiet house. Its wall provided adequate soundproofing against the noises from outside and they walked on a deep pile carpet that deadened any sound their feet might make. Paintings lit by low wattage spotlights lined the walls. Bernache suspected they might be by important artists but his knowledge of such things was limited.

They arrived at a carved teak door and Ruault knocked softly.

"Who's there?" Thierry Charrier sounded unexpectedly nervous.

162

"Pascal, with Inspector Monde."

"Send him in."

Ruault opened the door and the Inspector and Bernache entered the room. Unlike Samuel Prevost's study, this one was modern and functional, though a little out of date. Ruault did not enter the room, but closed it behind them.

Charrier was at the window looking out at his garden. In the distance, a gardener stood on a step ladder lopping branches from an overgrown bush. Charrier turned to face them and a smile played across his lips though it did not reach his eyes. He walked towards the Inspector and embraced him like a long lost friend.

"Charles, how good to see you. It has been many years since we last met and I see they have been kind to you. And you have brought a colleague with you?"

"This is Detective Bernache. He attends all my cases."

Charrier reached out with his hand and Bernache shook it. "Any friend of Charles is a friend of mine, though I cannot see how you might help. I have asked for Charles to assist me on a delicate family matter."

"Louis moves in the same world as I do, Thierry. Is this something to do with Gabrielle?"

Charrier waved his finger at the Inspector. "Always straight to the point, Charles. You haven't changed. Jacqueline would discuss the weather and the health of my family, but with you it was always business first and last."

"We are not here to discuss Jacqueline."

Charrier smiled again. "But in a way we are, Charles. You two were a formidable team who ran the Nazi's ragged. No other members of the Resistance came close to your many successes. The Nazi's put a large price on your heads. Then Jacqueline was captured and killed. You, acting alone, became even more formidable. We put it down to your desire for vengeance, but it wasn't only that was it? Does your boy here know how you achieved your successes?"

Bernache laughed and Charrier froze in surprise. "There are no secrets between the two of us, Monsieur Charrier. I know all about the Inspector's wife and the things they did together, before and after she died."

The Inspector worked hard to suppress a smile. "I told you, Thierry, we are a team. Gabrielle told you about Jacqueline? I'm surprised you believed her."

The smile had faded from Charrier's lips and he retreated behind his desk and sat down. "I didn't believe her. Gabrielle always had a fanciful streak and I thought she was amusing herself at my expense. That was before she came to my study last night and served me coffee. The back of her head was missing, Charles."

"What did she want?" Bernache asked.

Charrier slammed his fist down on the desk and snarled in anger. "She came to serve me coffee. Are you deaf as well as a fool?"

The Inspector was unimpressed by Charrier's anger and spoke calmingly.

"I suspect Detective Bernache was asking about her long term intent, Thierry. Not the excuse she used."

Charrier made a visible effort to calm himself. "I'm sorry, forgive my outburst. I don't know what she wants, which is why I called for you, Charles. Why has she waited ten years and what does she want?"

"Did she say anything else?"

"Only that she and the children would come and see me later. I waited up all night and nothing came. I want her soul to be at peace, Charles, and the souls of my children too."

"Ghosts do not manifest without reason, Monsieur Charrier," Bernache pointed out. "Is there a reason she might want to haunt you?"

Charrier turned his gaze on Bernache and his eyes were cold as ice. "I failed my wife and children, Detective. They were kidnapped and killed by Vincent Prevost. Only in France could I serve ten years in jail for ridding the world of such scum."

The Inspector pursed his lips.

"What exactly do you want us to do?"

Charrier sank back in his chair and sighed. "I want you to stay here until she returns, your boy as well if you want. Find out what she wants and set her soul at peace, Charles. You sent Jacqueline into the void when she was no longer needed, and I want you to do the same for Gabrielle."

Inspector Monde winced at Charrier's words, but he nodded his agreement. "I think it will be interesting to find out what Gabrielle wants and to point her on her way to heaven."

"I have had the bedroom next door to mine prepared for you. Is there anything else you want?"

"Detective Bernache will have to go out and get an overnight bag. I carry one in my car. I would like to look over the house and grounds, if you have no objection? It is useful to understand the lay of the land, so to speak."

"Whatever you want, Charles," Charrier said in clear dismissal.

VI

Pascal Ruault was waiting for them in the corridor outside. He led them back to the front door.

"The gates aren't locked, but you'll have to open and close them yourself," he informed Bernache once they had recovered the Inspector's overnight bag from the boot.

When Bernache had driven away, Ruault gestured that the Inspector should follow him. "I'll take you to your room."

"Thierry has agreed that I should familiarise myself with the house. Will you show me round?"

Ruault nodded sullenly. He looked uncomfortable and kept feeling the collar of his shirt as if it itched.

"Were you working for Thierry when his wife and children were kidnapped?"

The Inspector noted the fleeting look of discomfort that crossed Ruault's face.

"Yes. It was a bad time."

"And you were head of security back then, responsible for Madame Charrier's and the children's safety?"

"They kidnapped them while they were sleeping in the house. Monsieur Charrier, Serge and I were away on business in Leon. No one expected Prevost to try such a thing." Ruault stopped walking and faced the Inspector angrily. "I don't know why you're here, but that kidnapping was a long time ago and the man who did it is dead. I'm sure Monsieur Charrier did not summon you here to open old wounds."

The Inspector smiled apologetically. "You are quite right. It is the detective in me mixed with unforgiveable morbid curiosity. My wife knew Gabrielle well. They were friends during the war. Thierry must miss her dreadfully."

"It has been ten years," Ruault said shrugging as he spoke. He turned and led Monde to the floor above where the bedroom Charrier had allocated to him was located. The room had a feminine look to it, the dressing table was ornate and the faded wallpaper had once boasted bright flowers. There was a chaise longe positioned so that anyone seated on it could look across the garden through the window.

"Who's was this room? Was it Élise's?"

"This was Madame Charrier's room. Monsieur Charrier's room is through the connecting door and the children's rooms were on the other side of the corridor."

"Gabrielle and Thierry did not share a room?"

Ruault shrugged, but said nothing.

"Can I see the children's rooms?"

"Monsieur Charrier ordered them locked after his children were kidnapped. No one has been in them since and I don't have the keys."

"We must be close to Thierry's office below?" the Inspector enquired.

"There is a small flight of stairs linking his study to his bedroom."

The Inspector put his overnight bag on the bed. "Bernache will take the chair tonight. Now, Monsieur Ruault, show me around the house."

Once Inspector Monde had been shown everywhere in the house he decided to investigate the grounds. Ruault took his leave of him at the back door. A quick tour of the perimeter revealed that it was highly unlikely those responsible for the kidnap of Charrier's family could have entered or left the grounds by going over the wall.

Broken glass had been embedded into the wall not to mention an array of cast iron spikes made to look like decorations. Whoever had taken Gabrielle and her children must have used the gates. The police report into the kidnap was worse than useless. The investigating officers had concentrated solely on trying to find the victims, not on how they had been taken.

The gardens were a mess. Though superficially they looked well managed, on closer inspection the grass had bare patches and the trees, bushes and flower beds had been allowed to run wild. Monde's attention was drawn to a large conservatory. It was somewhere Ruault had not taken him when showing him around the house.

The conservatory was a two storey greenhouse attached to one side of the house. Several of its large panes of glass were cracked, but it was essentially sound.

The cast iron framed glass door swung open with a high pitched squeal when Monde pushed hard at it. Inside was a collection of tropical and sub-tropical plants. There were signs of recent restoration and new wire held long grape vines to the side of the wall. The door leading to the house was blocked behind a weave of vines and woody stems, though it looked as though someone was part way through cutting the door clear.

Against the house wall of the conservatory someone had recently created a bower of vines and underneath the bower was an unlikely sculpture. It looked brand new and it consisted of a group of people. In the centre of the group stood Thierry Charrier, large as life, if not slightly larger, in pure white alabaster. He had his left arm around his wife and his right around his two children. His wife and children sat on a bench while Thierry stood. Thierry smiled while the looks on his wife and children's faces were expressionless.

Monde found the tableau disturbing. When a hand touched him on the shoulder he jerked away as if the hand had been electrified.

"I'm sorry, monsieur. I did not mean to frighten you."

The man speaking was considerably older than Monde and wore old gardening clothing. Monde pulled himself together and addressed the man.

"I am Inspector Monde and you are…?"

167

The man took off his cap before answering. "Gaston Hiegel, the head gardener. Or rather I was when Madame Charrier was alive. They rehired me a few weeks ago to look after and restore the garden. I told him the work needed a team, but he said to do the best I could."

"He?"

"Monsieur Giraud." Gaston spat into the plants making his opinion of the man clear.

"You managed these gardens for Gabrielle? ...Forgive me, I mean Madame Charrier."

"You knew her?"

Monde shook his head. "Not well, my wife was friends with her during the war."

Gaston's eyes narrowed and then he came rushing at the Inspector, putting his arms around him and squeezing him hard.

"You are Charles Monde," Gaston said, releasing the Inspector to the point he could breathe. "I have always wanted to thank you. You freed my brother in a raid on a train bound for Auschwitz. You saved his life."

The Inspector gently extracted himself from the other's grip and the two men formally shook hands.

"You are here to finally get the bastards that killed Gabrielle, Élise and Nicolas?" Gaston asked.

"You do not think it was Prevost?"

Gaston spat again. "It was an inside job, Inspector. I went around the grounds the day after the kidnap and there was nothing out of place. There was not a footprint in the soil around the wall, nor the slightest sign of damage at the gates."

The Inspector looked shrewdly at the old man. "Who do you think was responsible?"

Gaston chose not to answer directly. "Madame and Monsieur Charrier were not as in-love as they had once been. But he loved his children and would not have hurt them, so it could not be him. Serge Giraud is a viper and Ruault would do anything asked of him. However, I'm afraid I do not know, Inspector."

"Serge Giraud is loyal to Charrier?"

"Loyal to his position as Charrier's second in command. I believe he would do anything to keep his place."

The Inspector nodded and returned his gaze to the group statue. "I did not think Thierry Charrier was so sentimental as to order such a thing and yet it must have been commissioned very recently. It looks brand new."

"No Inspector, it is ten years old. I found it in a crate not a dozen feet from where it now stands a few weeks ago. The delivery label was still attached. I believe Madame Charrier must have commissioned it just before she was kidnapped. I like it because it is so lifelike and reminds me of her and the children."

"I find it disturbing for some reason. But it does look like her and the artist has captured Thierry perfectly. The others look a little out of proportion don't you think?"

Gaston considered the group. "You know you are right, Inspector. I hadn't noticed it before."

VII

The evening meal was a quiet and sullen occasion. Charrier didn't speak. Ruault and Giraud took their cue from their boss and were equally silent. The Inspector appeared lost in thought and Bernache's attempts to start a conversation was met with grunts or silence.

The meal, however, was excellent and the maid who served them was quick and efficient. Despite this, Bernache was happy to see the end of it. The men sat around the table drinking brandy and Charrier lit a cigar.

"Your plans for the night?" the Inspector enquired.

"I shall work in my bedroom," Charrier replied. "If anything happens I shall call to you."

Giraud looked annoyed. "I can stay with you if you're expecting trouble, boss. You don't need the police." He managed to make the word *police* sound like a euphemism for something foul.

"The kind of trouble I'm expecting cannot be dealt with your way, or even the police way, Serge. Charles is an old friend with special skills."

169

"If I'm not needed, I shall retire to my room," Giraud stood and left without waiting for a reply.

Ruault stood up and pushed away his chair. "I should check the grounds."

Charrier nodded absently and Ruault hurried from the room.

The Inspector smiled and sipped at his brandy. "It seems your men are upset by the presence of policemen at your table."

"I haven't told them about Gabrielle. I don't wish to appear crazy. They don't understand why you're here."

Charrier stood. "I'm going to my room. Don't spend too long down here. I don't wish to face Gabrielle alone." He left the room leaving Bernache and the Inspector facing each other across the table.

"If this is the typical life of a crime lord I'm glad I'm just a lowly detective," Bernache pointed out. "The brandy is excellent though."

It was a little past eleven when a garden scythe flew at walking speed through the house and up the stairs until it reached Thierry Charrier's room. It positioned itself against the wall of the corridor and became still.

Pascal Ruault was making his last circuit of the grounds before going to bed. He checked that the gates were securely padlocked and then walked back to house. The front door was ajar, which was unexpected and he stopped and listened, hearing nothing but the normal sounds of the night.

"If one of our guests has gone out walking he's going to find it difficult to get back inside," he said to himself and smiled at the thought of one of the policemen spending the night outside. He stepped into the house, locking and bolting the door securely behind him.

His next job was to check that all the windows on the ground floor were closed. Ruault had just finished that task when Gabrielle and her children appeared in front of him. The children had neat bullet holes through their foreheads and it was the holes that held his attention as they smiled at him.

"Pascal, there are some questions we have to ask you," Gabrielle said. "We've been waiting a long time for the chance."

Pascal Ruault was considered a brave man by those who knew him and they would have been surprised at his high pitched scream and the way he turned and ran. Gabrielle vanished as her children ran after the terrified man.

There was a choice of directions when he reached the stairs. Gabrielle appeared in the corridor, leaving only the stairs. She smiled warmly and held out a hand to him. Ruault looked back and his blood ran cold at what he saw. The children didn't look like children anymore. Their mouths had grown to an impossible size to accommodate sharp tearing teeth with blood dripping from their fangs. He ran up the stairs as fast as his legs would carry him.

Ruault ran down the corridor past the Inspector's room and slid to a stop as Gabrielle appeared in front of him with her palm raised.

"My children will deal with you here," she said, a faint smile on her lips.

Ruault turned back the way he had come to face the children, now looking much like they had the day they died, if you discounted the bullet holes.

Élise picked up the scythe she had placed there earlier and hefted it.

"Gaston is a good gardener. He always cleans his tools and keeps them nice and sharp."

Ruault pulled himself together with a struggle and when he spoke he barely stammered. "You're just a ghost. Ghosts can't hurt people."

"Show him," Nicolas urged, an evil grin on his face.

Élise swung the scythe and ripped an expensive painting on the wall into two.

"Lots of practice," she said with a touch of pride in her voice.

Ruault felt his feet leave the ground and seconds later he was lying horizontal up near the ceiling, looking down on a scythe that was being held in a position to cut his throat should he fall. He screamed.

"Who were you working for?" Élise asked sweetly. "That's all we want to know, and when you tell us, we'll let you go."

Gabrielle opened the door to her husband's bedroom and stepped inside, leaving it ajar. He was working at his desk in pyjamas and dressing gown.

"Where have you been?" she asked and he turned towards her. "We've been waiting for you for such a long time and look, you've grown old."

"Monde! She's here!" Charrier yelled.

A scream sounded in the corridor and Gabrielle smiled at her husband, showing her teeth. "That's the children getting answers. Don't worry about it."

The Inspector and Bernache were sitting at a table playing cards when they heard Charrier's yell. They had barely got to their feet when they heard a chilling scream from the same direction.

"Mon Dieu. She's killing him," Bernache said in horror as they ran towards the connecting door. They tumbled through it to find Charrier and his wife standing some distance from each other. Charrier was unharmed.

Gabrielle turned to look at them. "Charles, how good to see you, you look so old."

"Gabrielle, this is not the way." The Inspector held his hands out to her.

Gabrielle looked puzzled. "It's difficult to hold onto things. I couldn't have remembered you until you appeared." Her face took on an anguished look. "We need to know, Charles. We need to know why we died."

"Vengeance is not worth the price," Bernache said.

There were sounds of voices in the corridor. Suddenly a voice yelled out in terror, "I'll tell you. We were…"

A gun shot sounded outside bringing the conversation to a halt. It was followed by the sound of something heavy hitting the floor. Gabrielle vanished.

The Inspector and Bernache ran to the open door and Bernache looked cautiously out. He nodded to the Inspector and stepped into the corridor.

Ruault lay on the floor his feet nearest to them. His head lay severed from his body, a few inches beyond it. There was the faint smell of gun-smoke in the air though the corridor was deserted.

Ruault's head slid forward a few inches and then lifted into the air. It flew towards Bernache; face first, mouth open and gaping. When it reached him it rotated down so that the crown of the head became visible, revealing a neat bullet hole through the top of the skull.

172

A little boy's voice came from the air, next to the head.

"See, it wasn't us. We didn't do it."

The head fell to the floor and Bernache jumped out of the way as it bounced towards him.

"I don't suppose you did," the Inspector remarked dryly.

VIII

"**W**hat happened?" Charrier asked from the door. He stared at the body on the floor. "Did Nicolas and Élise do this?"

"No, Serge Giraud shot him first," the Inspector said grimly. "Ruault was about to tell your children who was behind their murders. We must get to Giraud before they do."

Monde turned over the headless corpse and took Ruault's gun from its holster. He waved it grip first at Bernache.

"You'd better take this, Louis. I hate guns."

Bernache shook his head and took a snub nose revolver from his pocket. "I felt it best to come armed." The Inspector nodded and put Ruault's gun in his pocket.

"I don't understand. Vincent Prevost shot my children," Charrier said calmly despite the decapitation in front of him. He seemed to have fully recovered and was almost nonchalant. He put his right hand into his dressing gown casually as if checking he was carrying something.

A high pitched scream coming from the floor below stopped any further conversation and the Inspector and Bernache ran down the corridor with Charrier trailing behind them.

They found a maid in her nightclothes on the ground floor. She was sitting against the wall with her hands over her mouth. She looked terrified.

"Which way?" Bernache asked and she pointed down the corridor.

The Inspector stopped and put a hand on the maid's shoulder as Charrier and Bernache went on ahead.

"Find the other servants and tell them to stay in their rooms until I say it is safe for them to come out." When he was sure the maid had understood, Monde followed after the others.

There was an open door at the end of the corridor. It led out to the conservatory. The vines that had been blocking the door were gone and a light switch was now visible on the wall. The inspector threw the switch and the conservatory lit up around him. He nodded in satisfaction as he hadn't expected Gaston to be so thorough in so short a time.

Bernache and Charrier had come to a halt a few feet in front of him. As Monde joined them he saw what had stopped them. Serge Giraud was hanging in the air, about half a metre off the ground surrounded by three very angry ghosts.

"Tell us who gave you your orders," Élise said angrily, her fists were clenched and she stamped the floor in frustration.

"Can I take him to the roof and drop him, Mummy?" Nicolas asked. He had his hands raised as if it were he holding Giraud suspended.

Gabrielle shushed her children and faced Giraud. "You executed us, Serge. Don't deny it because we remember it as though it was minutes ago. It seems you never forget your own death."

Giraud gave Charrier a pleading look, but Charrier was staring at him as if he had never seen him before.

"Vincent Prevost killed my children. You told me that, Serge," Charrier said.

Élise turned towards her father. "He shot me just after he shot Mummy. The end of the pistol was still hot enough to burn my forehead before he pulled the trigger."

"How could you know? Weren't you blindfolded?" her Father asked her incredulously.

"I'd taken off the blindfold and I was looking in *his* eyes when he pulled the trigger!"

Gabrielle saw her husband's anger building and took Nicolas's hand. Giraud dropped to the floor.

"Let your father deal with him, dear," she said quietly.

"You killed my children," Charrier shouted at Giraud.

"I had no choice. Élise recognised me and Prevost had found us," Giraud said desperately. "He would have used them to destroy me."

Charrier advanced and Giraud pulled out his gun. "Stay away from me, boss. I'll shoot."

Gabrielle and her children stepped further back leaving the two men to sort out their differences. Charrier kept walking and Giraud fired a warning shot. Monde and Bernache dived for cover as the round came perilously close to them.

"You'll have to do better than that," Charrier said in an ice cold voice. "I trusted you and you betrayed me."

"Boss, I wouldn't have told. Samuel Prevost tried to blackmail me and I refused to work for him. You know I'm loyal."

Charrier's face contorted in anger. "Shut up! You killed my children."

He took another step closer and Giraud shot again. Charrier looked down at his leg in surprise as a dark stain appeared on his pyjamas and began to spread. He fell to the floor, pulling a gun from his pocket and firing five shots into Giraud's chest. Giraud fell to the floor, a look of surprise on his face as he died.

Monde and Bernache got up from behind the massive plant pots they'd been hiding behind and walked towards Charrier. He was holding his leg at the place where the bullet had entered. Gabrielle and her children moved towards Charrier from the other side, there was nothing friendly about the way they looked.

"Stop them, Monde," Charrier called out desperately. "I didn't do anything. It wasn't my fault."

"Louis, staunch Thierry's wound," the Inspector commanded and hurried passed Charrier towards the three ghosts.

"He arranged it, Charles," Gabrielle said loudly. "You heard what Serge said."

"You can't know for sure," the Inspector said soothingly. "Do you want the burden of killing an innocent man on your children's souls?"

"I was brought up believing in an eye for an eye," Gabrielle said angrily. "It's what Jacqueline would have done."

"Let us talk."

The Inspector led the ghosts away from Charrier and Bernache and out of earshot. He spoke urgently to Gabrielle and her children and Bernache saw him waving his arms to emphasise his words.

175

Bernache took Charrier's dressing gown's belt and used it to bind his wound.

"It's only a flesh wound," he told Charrier. "You'll live."

"I always do," Charrier said, wincing as the belt was tightened. "I've been shot before by better men than Serge Giraud. I'm a born survivor, Detective."

Charrier's eyes were drawn to the statue group under the bower. His eyes widened in surprise. "That thing is hideous," he said. "How did it get in my garden?"

Bernache looked at the group and shrugged. "This is your conservatory, Monsieur. It's no use asking me."

Charrier had turned his attention back to the ghosts of his family and the Inspector. They were no longer arguing and it seemed to Charrier that his wife looked happier and he saw his children's ghosts were grinning.

"Charles always does the right thing, no matter how foolish it is," he said, more to himself than Bernache. "I knew I could rely on him."

"The Inspector never does anything foolish, Monsieur. You will see."

Inspector Monde walked back to the two men, leaving the ghosts standing where they were.

"They have agreed to move on," he said wearily. "Their kidnappers are dead and justice has been done. I have told them it is best they make no personal goodbyes, but they will depart when you wave at them."

Charrier grinned and struggled to sit up. He looked at his wife and children and waved cheerfully in their direction. All three vanished.

"It is that easy to get rid of ghosts, Charles? They are gone for good?"

The Inspector sighed. "They know their vengeance is complete. They have moved on to a better place."

Charrier laughed cynically. "Then your job is done. Call my servants and go."

The Inspector looked down at Charrier with open contempt. "You ordered Giraud to kidnap your wife and children, but he was only supposed to kill Gabrielle, wasn't he?"

Charrier seemed amused by Monde's question. "I had tired of her and she had served her purpose by bearing my children. I

176

always intended to kill Prevost and her death was to provide the excuse. But her body went missing and I served ten years in prison. A miscalculation on my part, but you'll never prove it, Charles."

"You have just confessed in front of two police officers," Bernache said in open disgust.

"As if any jury would believe you," Charrier said and laughed again. "I will tell you something to show what a fool Charles is. All those years ago during the war, I sold him and his wife out to the Nazis. They only caught her, but they paid me plenty for the information. He kept on working with me afterwards. That made it all especially delicious."

Bernache pulled his gun out of his pocket and pointed it at Charrier. "I will kill him for you, Inspector. Just give me the word."

Monde was staring at nothing, his gaze not on this world or in this place. His face was ashen. He waved a hand at Bernache. "Put the gun away, Louis."

Charrier had looked frightened when Bernache pulled the gun, but he recovered as soon as the Inspector spoke.

"You're a weak man, Charles. You always were, for all your brave acts and good deeds. A weak man and a fool."

The Inspector pointed at the statues in the bower. "Have you noticed them, Thierry? Gaston told me you never visit the garden and the door to the conservatory was blocked until he cleared it today. He cleared it at my request."

"It's sentimental rubbish. Gabrielle was always buying things like that."

"No, it was not Gabrielle. That is a gift from Vincent Prevost. It didn't arrive until after you shot him, but it was commissioned the day he found the bodies of your family. Prevost had a sense of irony unusual in a criminal and plaster can look very like stone if it is painted by an artist."

Charrier felt the hairs on the back of his neck rise. He stared at the statues and his wife and children's eyes snapped open. Blood ran down the statues' white cheeks like tears.

"What is happening?" Charrier asked anxiously. He began to drag himself towards the door into the house, his wounded leg slowing him down.

"I lied to you earlier. I told your family they could not extract revenge unless they had proof it was you who arranged the kidnapping. Gabrielle and your children agreed to wait until you confessed. Now it is time for you to confront them in the flesh."

The Inspector stepped back and pulled Bernache away so they were no longer between the statues and Charrier.

The three statues began to crack and thin pieces of plaster fell away. Gabrielle and her children stood and large chunks of plaster hit the stone floor and scattered. What remained was hideous. Rotted flesh came away with the plaster revealing sinews and bones beneath, preserved in the airless environment of their plaster tombs.

Charrier tried to crawl away, but Gabrielle caught up with him and pushed him so he lay on his back on the floor.

"This is your father, children," she said through a mouth that was all teeth and jaw bone, her lips and face having been lost with the plaster. "You should always kiss your father when you haven't seen him for a while. Let me show you how."

She knelt beside her husband and he cringed as their faces met. A second later he screamed in agony.

Gabrielle lifted her head to look at her children. Fresh blood covered her sinews and ran down between her teeth. She spat out her husband's nose contemptuously.

"Do you see how it is done?" she asked them as if she had been showing her children how to sip tea.

"I think I can do that, Mummy," Élise said and clacked her teeth together in anticipation. "And Daddy has such lovely arms."

"I want a leg," Nicolas said and dived onto his father ahead of Élise. The girl laughed and fell to her knees in front of her father.

Gabrielle put her head down again as her husband's screams intensified.

The four bodies jerked for minutes and then they were still.

"You were wrong, Louis," the Inspector said as they stared at the bloody ruin on the floor.

"About what, Inspector?"

"You said that vengeance isn't worth the price, but I feel it has been well worth it today.

The End

178

ABOUT THE AUTHOR

John Booth has been writing ghost and horror stories for over five years. Inspector Monde is his favourite character, but he doesn't find it easy to write about him as he's determined to keep the quality high and finding appropriate stories lines for Inspector Monde doesn't happen every day.

John is happily married with two grown up daughters and a young grandson. He lives quietly in England and rarely meets ghosts, but is always polite to them when he does. For most of his life he has been a consultant engineer. He's never been too sure how to describe what that job title actually means, except to say that it has never involved grease guns or getting his hands dirty.

From Pfoxmoor Publishing

A Young Adult Fantasy-Adventure
WIZARDS by John Booth

Being a teenager is tough enough. Growing up different, with a secret that no one will understand, gets Jake noticed by the cops. Jake finds missing people, most times too late and the cops are suspicious.

Jake discovered his secret by accident—a hopscotch court that takes him to other worlds and other times. He uses that power reluctantly, feeling confused and out of his depth. But one good thing comes of it—he discovers a new best friend, a dragon. And his girlfriend, Jenny.

But nothing's ever simple. Evil wizards, kingdoms at war, chases, rescues, an offer he can't refuse… and a princess who seems to know his every move. Princess Esmeralda has an agenda and his girlfriend does not approve.

Jake is a wizard and his life is about to get interesting.

Rave Reviews for Wizards:

"Author John Booth writes with a light touch, so gentle you barely feel his presence. The book paints many lovely, lyrical scenes..."
—Barbara Silkstone, Amazon review

"Wizards is an entertaining, funny, light-hearted and serious look at growing up into your own powers, be it mind, magic or muscle, something that many teenagers will be able to empathize with."
—The Tiger Princess Reviews

In print and eBook
www.pfoxmoorpublishing.com

Coming Fall 2011

WIZARDS WEDDING by John Booth

The adventure continues...

Jake is in trouble. Sure, he's in jail suspected of kidnapping and killing a little girl, but he discounts that. The little girl in question is a dangerous wizard with homicidal tendencies currently enjoying herself on another world, but Jake can't tell the police that. However, that problem is in the noise as far as he's concerned.

The real problem worrying him is that he cheated on Jenny with Princess Esmeralda and he knows he's no good at lying. Jenny's the love of his life and he's terrified of losing her. Hiding in jail suits him fine while he figures out what to do.

Jake thinks he has problems now, but the ones waiting in the wings are far bigger. He's going to be tested to the limit as he faces deadly enemies on all sides. And his problems with Jenny and Esmeralda are just beginning.

From Pfoxchase Publishing

THE SPARROW CONUNDRUM

A Dark Comedy by Bill Kirton

North Sea oil is drying up.

In Aberdeen, several shadowy organisations struggle to get a share of the action in offshore contracts: Eagle with his deputies Hawk and Kestrel and his bearded secretary Mary; the Belazzo boys; the Russians; and one other mysterious outfit.

Chris Machin (code name Sparrow) helped the Belazzos when he was a student; now it's payback time and he's scared. When his garden explodes, he turns to Eagle for help.

Then there's his ex-girlfriend, Tessa, her boss Big Snake and, worst of all, a sociopathic police inspector called Lodgedale. The resolution of the various plots involves a power struggle, two wrestlers, a trip to Inverness, a fishing trawler and several murders. The identity of the Big Snake is revealed, Tessa is promoted, and goodies and baddies alike get what they most desire.

Oh, all except Machin.

Action-Fantasy-Adventure

SPAR WITH THE DEVIL
BOOK ONE: PORTALS

A Sweeping Saga of Betrayal and Desire from
T.S. Bond

Portals—gateways to dangerous inter-dimensional worlds—provide refuge for a culture under siege and the last hope for two strangers united by a quirk of fate.

To save her he must destroy her spirit…

Asgeirr must break Caitlin's spirit if they are to survive the savage predators and the endless night … and the rival groups pursuing them relentlessly.

…for her secrets may lead them both into bondage.

Bound by fear and conflicting loyalties, Caitlin must learn to master her talents and discover the man behind the demon mask—the man who risks all to keep her safe.

In eBook and Print from Amazon and other fine retailers.

www.pfoxchase.com

The Saga Continues

COMING FALL 2011

THE DEVIL AND THE FALCON
BOOK TWO: PORTALS

A Sweeping Saga of Betrayal and Desire from
T.S. Bond

The saga continues as Ásgeirr and Caitlin struggle against lies,
half-truths and clever distortions that tear them apart.
Without his mate, Ásgeirr has nothing to live for until he discovers
Caitlin"s brother, a trained killer and drug addict, held in thrall by
Gunnarr, the head of Greyfalcon. He joins forces with Caitlin"s
father to bring down the Greyfalcon organization and rescue
Kieran from a life of ruin and despair.

Caitlin learns that the three people who matter most to her now
work for Greyfalcon. Her feelings for Ásgeirr are complicated.
Love, hate, and desire war with her need to right wrongs as she
travels a torturous path where no one can be trusted and deceit is a
way of life.

Caitlin had sparred with the Devil alone but now she has a companion
in her quest—and his name is Wolf, the decorated captain of the
Althing forces and the man she learns to trust with her life, and
possibly her heart.